Anglais 5e

Nadine Beaulieu
Christiane Dupuy
professeurs d'anglais

Illustrations
David Scrima

TACTIC

avec les conseils de Brigitte Prot

Albin Michel
ÉDUCATION

SOMMAIRE

LES PRONOMS

LES ADJECTIFS

LE NOM, L'ARTICLE

LA POSSESSION

FRÉQUENCE ET DURÉE

LES QUANTIFICATEURS

LES PRÉPOSITIONS

LES NOMBRES

ABRÉVIATIONS

aux. : auxiliaire
GB : en anglais
interrog. : interrogatif
pers. : personne
pron. : pronom
sing. singulier
US : en américain
v : verbe

INTRODUCTION

Cet ouvrage est conforme au programme d'anglais en 5e. Il rassemble les bases de grammaire, de vocabulaire et d'expression écrite que tu dois avoir assimilées à la fin de l'année scolaire.

TACTIC se présente sous forme de fiches aisément identifiables à utiliser dans l'ordre ou en choisissant les points précis que tu as besoin de revoir. Chaque fiche comporte un point essentiel du programme, résumé de façon simple, et des exercices d'application pour lesquels tu peux t'aider du vocabulaire du lexique.

Les corrigés, complets et accessibles, permettent une vérification immédiate de tes réponses. Parfois accompagnés de précisions et d'explications supplémentaires, ils constituent aussi un approfondissement.

Grâce aux exercices, tu peux vérifier immédiatement ta compréhension de la leçon, t'entraîner et progresser facilement.

Tu peux utiliser TACTIC **après un cours** pour faire le point et remédier à tes éventuelles difficultés, **avant un contrôle** pour réviser tes connaissances, **pendant les vacances** pour te préparer à l'entrée en 4e.

Bon courage !

Les auteurs

Mode d'emploi
Replie d'abord les corrigés de manière à n'avoir sous les yeux que la partie « règle » et les énoncés. Une fois tes exercices terminés, relève la partie « corrigés » et compare avec tes réponses.

LES CONSEILS DE BRIGITTE PROT

pour bien réussir son année

Te voici au début d'un nouveau «cycle» qui comprend les classes de 5e et de 4e. Ça devient sérieux !
En anglais, l'année de 5e te permet :
- d'approfondir ce que tu as appris l'an dernier,
- d'acquérir les connaissances qui te préparent à la classe de 4e.

Tu apprendras à t'exprimer, à l'oral et à l'écrit, sur des sujets de plus en plus intéressants.
Pour y parvenir, tu travailleras le vocabulaire, la grammaire, la phonologie (l'étude des sons) et la civilisation.

■ Pour réussir cette année, voici neuf conseils :

1. Ne dis pas : «L'anglais en 5e, c'est trop difficile : je n'y arriverai pas ! ».
Cette phrase est l'ennemie de ta motivation, elle t'empêche de progresser.
Avant de te mettre au travail, regarde toujours ce que tu sais déjà
et ce que tu as à apprendre, sans dramatiser !

2. Si tu rencontres une difficulté, dans une leçon ou un exercice, demande à tes parents de t'aider.
Ne garde pas de question sans réponse.

3. Ne te décourage pas à la première mauvaise note !
Regarde, comprends tes erreurs, puis corrige-les. Ainsi, à la prochaine interrogation, tu auras toutes les chances d'obtenir un meilleur résultat.

4. Dans ton travail, repère d'abord ce que tu as appris en 6e.
Cela te donne un «point d'appui» pour développer ta confiance en toi.

5. Utilise une méthode de travail simple et efficace.
Suis les conseils de ton professeur et de tes parents. TACTIC peut t'aider à bien retenir la leçon pour réussir les exercices en peu de temps.

6. Respecte ton emploi du temps dans la semaine.
Tu dois le répartir entre le travail, le sport et les temps «libres».
Tu en as besoin pour ton équilibre.

7. Apprends à te concentrer dans ton travail personnel.
Fixe-toi un temps limité. Par exemple, tu dis : «Je ferai ma rédaction de 16 heures à 16 heures 30, mercredi», et non : «Je commencerai ma rédaction à 16 heures, et je verrai bien quand j'aurai fini !»

8. Entraîne-toi régulièrement aux exercices.
Ensuite, montre-les à tes parents. Parfois, fais-les avec eux. Ainsi, ils pourront repérer tes progrès : cela t'encouragera à poursuivre tes efforts.

9. Écoute les personnes qui te donnent envie de travailler.
N'écoute pas celles qui te découragent.

En anglais, cette année t'offre des découvertes intéressantes.
TACTIC t'accompagnera dans cette «aventure» !

Brigitte PROT

SE PRÉSENTER
What's your name? : Quel est ton / votre nom ?
My name's Sylvia : Mon nom est Sylvia.

Where are you from? : D'où es-tu / êtes-vous ?
I'm from Ireland / I am Irish : Je suis d'Irlande / Je suis irlandaise
How old are you? : Quel âge as-tu / avez-vous ?
I'm fifteen / I'm fifteen years old : J'ai 15 ans.

How are you? : Comment vas-tu / allez-vous ?
I'm fine : Je vais bien.

What are you? : Que faites-vous dans la vie?
I'm a student : Je suis étudiant(e).

EXERCICE 1

a) How **are** you? I **am** fine, thanks, and you?
(➜ *Pour dire que l'on va bien en anglais, on utilise l'auxiliaire* be.)

b) **Is** Jorge Portuguese? No, he **is** Spanish.

c) **Are** they very old? No, they **are** only 50.

d) How old **is** Keith? He **is** thirteen.

EXERCICE 2

a) I am in ??????
Where **are you**?

b) My sister is surprised because ??????
Why **is your sister surprised**?

c) My parents are angry because we ??????
Why **are your parents angry**?

EXERCICE 3

a) Terry is Dutch.
Terry isn't Dutch.
(➜ *L'adjectif de nationalité prend une majuscule en anglais.*)

b) I am fifteen.
I'm not fifteen.
(➜ *Pour dire son âge en anglais, on utilise l'auxiliaire* be.)

c) Paul and Lisa are married.
Paul and Lisa aren't married.

EXERCICE 4

a) Caterina is Greek.
Caterina's Greek.

b) My aunt is not thirty.
My aunt isn't thirty.

c) They are lawyers.
They're lawyers.

d) I am not a student.
I'm not a student.
(➜ *En anglais, devant les noms de profession au singulier, il faut mettre l'article* a.)

1 *BE* AU PRÉSENT SIMPLE

- **L'auxiliaire *be* au présent.**

I am, you are, she / he / it is ; we are, you are, they are.

- **Questions.**

Be + sujet
Are they tired?

- **Phrases négatives.**

Sujet + *be* + *not*
She is not happy.

- **Se présenter.**

I am Sandra, I am French.

- **Dire son âge.**

I am 13.

- **Formes contractées .**

I'm ; you're ; she's / he's / it's ; we're ; you're, they're.
I'm not ; you aren't, she / he / it isn't ;
we / you / they aren't.

1. Complète les phrases à l'aide de *be* conjugué au présent simple.

a) How .... you?

I .... fine, thanks, and you?

b) .... Jorge Portuguese?

No, he .... Spanish.

c) .... they very old?

No, they .... only 50.

d) How old .... Keith?

He .... thirteen.

2. Tu parles avec Peter au téléphone. La ligne est mauvaise. Pose des questions sur les informations que tu n'entends pas.

a) I am in ??????

Where ....?

b) My sister is surprised because ????

Why ....?

c) My parents are angry because we ???

Why ....?

3. Mets les phrases à la forme négative. Utilise la forme contractée.

a) Terry is Dutch.

....

b) I am fifteen.

....

c) Paul and Lisa are married.

....

4. Réécris les phrases en mettant le verbe à la forme contractée.

a) Caterina is Greek.

....

b) My aunt is not thirty.

....

c) They are lawyers.

....

d) I am not a student.

....

VOCABULAIRE

to be cold : avoir froid
to be hot : avoir très chaud
to be hungry : avoir faim
to be right : avoir raison
to be thirsty : avoir soif
to be warm : avoir chaud
to be wrong : avoir tort

it's cold : il fait froid
it's warm : il fait chaud
it's hot : il fait très chaud
it's windy : il y a du vent
it's sunny : il y a du soleil
it's early : il est tôt
it's late : il est tard

Attention !
N'oublie pas que certaines expressions qui se construisent avec l'auxiliaire *avoir* en français, se traduisent en anglais avec l'auxiliaire *be.*

Ex. : avoir froid = to be cold.

EXERCICE 1

tall	short
right	wrong
happy	sad
interesting	boring
small	big
dark-haired	light-haired
fat	thin

EXERCICE 2

a) Let's not eat now. I am not **hungry**.

b) My teacher is very **angry** because we never do our homework.

c) Could I have a glass of ice-tea? I am so **thirsty**.

d) Take light clothes with you; it will be very **warm** in Africa.

EXERCICE 3

a) Tom is **tall** **(Tom's tall)**.

b) **He is happy** **(He's happy)**.

c) **He is dark-haired** **(He's dark-haired)**.

d) **He is thin** **(He's thin)**.

EXERCICE 4

a) Avez-vous froid ?
Are you cold?

b) Je ne suis pas gros.
I am not fat (I'm not fat).

c) Elle a très soif.
She is very thirsty (She's very thirsty).

2 *BE* ET LES ADJECTIFS

- **Décrire quelqu'un.**
  He is tall ; she is dark-haired.
- **Décrire quelque chose.**
  It's big.
- **Parler d'un état.**
  I am happy ; she is angry.
- **Dire que l'on a chaud ou froid, faim ou soif.**
  I am cold / warm.
  We are hungry / thirsty.
- **Parler du temps qu'il fait.**
  It's hot ; it's windy.
- **Donner une opinion.**
  It's interesting ; it's boring.

1. Relie par une flèche chaque adjectif et son contraire.

tall ▪	▪ boring
right ▪	▪ big
happy ▪	▪ wrong
interesting ▪	▪ thin
small ▪	▪ short
dark-haired ▪	▪ sad
fat ▪	▪ light-haired

2. Complète les phrases à l'aide des adjectifs suivants : ***warm - thirsty - hungry - angry.***

a) Let's not eat now. I am not ....

b) My teacher is very .... because we never do our homework.

c) Could I have a glass of ice-tea?

I am so ....

d) Take light clothes with you;

it will be very .... in Africa.

3. Trouve quatre adjectifs, dans l'exercice 1, pour décrire Tom. Compose quatre phrases.

a) Tom is ....

....

b) ....

....

c) ....

....

d) ....

4. Comment dirais-tu en anglais ?

a) Avez-vous froid ?

....

b) Je ne suis pas gros.

....

c) Elle a très soif.

....

EXERCICE 1

a) Jane **has got** a suitcase.

b) Jane **has not got** gloves.

c) Peter **has got** a tie.

d) They **have got** shoes.

EXERCICE 2

a) She has got a new pair of shoes.
Has she got a new pair of shoes?
What has she got?

b) Mark and Mary have got a lot of clothes.
Have Mark and Mary got a lot of clothes?
What have they got?

c) They have got leather boots.
Have they got leather boots?
What have they got?

EXERCICE 3

a) Cynthia has got a computer.
Cynthia**'s got** a computer.

b) She has not got an answer phone.
She **hasn't got** an answer phone.

c) I have got a camera.
I**'ve got** a camera.

FORMES CONTRACTÉES

Phrases affirmatives

I have got = I've got
you have got = you've got
he / she / it has got = he's / she's / it's got
we have got = we've got
they have got = they've got

Phrases négatives

I have not got = I haven't got
you have not got = you haven't got
he / she / it has not got = he / she / it hasn't got
we have not got = we haven't got
they have not got = they haven't got

3

HAVE GOT

- **Parler de ce que l'on possède au présent.**

I / you / we / they + have got
he / she / it + has got
She has got a parrot.

- **Questions.**

Have / has + sujet + *got*
Have you got time?

- **Phrases négatives.**

Sujet + *have / has + not + got*
She has not got a car.

- **Parler de soi.**

I have got blue eyes and long hair.

1. Complète les phrases. Dis ce que Peter et Jane ont ou n'ont pas.

a) Jane .... a suitcase.

b) Jane .... gloves.

c) Peter .... a tie.

d) They .... shoes.

2. Pose des questions sur les mots soulignés.

Ex. : We have got a raincoat.
Have we got a raincoat? ou
What have we got?

a) She has got a new pair of shoes.

....?

....?

b) Mark and Mary have got a lot of clothes.

....?

....?

c) They have got leather boots.

....?

....?

3. Écris les verbes des phrases suivantes à la forme contractée.

a) Cynthia has got a computer.

....

b) She has not got an answer phone.

....

c) I have got a camera.

....

EXERCICE 1

a) Are you late, Jane?
Yes, I am. Yes, I'm.
(➜ *La réponse courte ne se contracte pas à la forme affirmative.)*

b) Has Terry got a sofa?
No, he hasn't. No, he haven't.
(➜ Have *au présent simple devient* has *à la troisième personne du singulier.)*

c) Is the radio on?
Yes, it are. **Yes, it is.**

d) Have the Beavers got a trailor?
No, they haven't. No, they have'nt.

EXERCICE 2

a) Is Hans Dutch?
No, he **isn't**.

b) Are you sick?
Yes, I **am**.

c) Have they got birds?
Yes, they **have**.

d) Have we got sugar?
No, we **haven't**.

e) Am I right?
No, you **aren't**.

➜ *Les réponses courtes ne se contractent qu'à la forme négative* !

EXERCICE 3

a) Are you good at mathematics?
Yes, I **am**.

b) Is your friend English?
No, he **is not (isn't)**.

c) Are your parents at home?
No, they **are not (aren't)**.

d) Have you got brothers and sisters?
Yes, I **have**.

e) Has your friend got a brother?
No, he **has not (hasn't)**.

RÉPONSES COURTES

To be	*Yes, I am*	*No, I am not (I'm not)*
	you are	*you are not (you aren't)*
	he is	*he is not (he isn't)*
	she is	*she is not (she isn't)*
	it is	*it is not (it isn't)*
	we are	*we are not (we aren't)*
	they are	*they are not (they aren't)*
To have	*Yes, I have*	*No, I have not (I haven't)*
	you have	*you have not (you haven't)*
	he has	*he has not (he hasn't)*
	she has	*she has not (she hasn't)*
	it has	*it has not (it hasn't)*
	we have	*we have not (we haven't)*
	they have	*they have not (they haven't)*

4 *BE* ET *HAVE* – RÉPONSES COURTES

● **Emploi.**

On les utilise pour répondre à une question sans reprendre toute la phrase.

● **Formation.**

Sujet + auxiliaire *be* ou *have.*
Are you Swedish? No, I'm not.
Êtes-vous Suédois ? Non, je ne le suis pas.
Have we got water? Yes, we have.
Avons-nous de l'eau ? Oui, nous en avons.

● **Attention !**

Les réponses courtes ne se contractent qu'à la forme négative.
Yes, I am ; you / we / they are ; he / she / it is.
No, I'm not ; you / we / they aren't ; he / she / it isn't.
Yes, I / you / we / they have; he / she / it has.
No, I / we / you / they haven't ; he / she / it hasn't.

1. Parmi les deux réponses proposées, souligne celle qui est correcte.

a) Are you late, Jane?
Yes, I am. Yes, I'm.

b) Has Terry got a sofa?
No, he hasn't. No, he haven't.

c) Is the radio on?
Yes, it are. Yes, it is.

d) Have the Beavers got a trailor?
No, they haven't. No, they have'nt.

2. Écris la forme contractée des réponses courtes.
Attention, certaines ne se contractent pas !

a) Is Hans Dutch? No, he is not.

....

b) Are you sick? Yes, I am.

....

c) Have they got birds? Yes, they have.

....

d) Have we got sugar? No, we have not.

....

e) Am I right? No, you are not.

....

3. Réponds aux questions de ton professeur.

a) Are you good at mathematics?

Yes, I ....

b) Is your friend English?

No, he ....

c) Are your parents at home?

No, they ....

d) Have you got brothers and sisters?

Yes, I ....

e) Has your friend got a brother?

No, he ....

EXERCICE 1

a) She is tall, ... ?
forme **négative**

b) The baker hasn't got a daughter, ...?
forme **affirmative**

c) You aren't my friend, ...?
forme **affirmative**

d) Your cousins have got a CD player ...?
forme **négative**

EXERCICE 2

a) He is your brother,
isn't he? is he?

b) This letter isn't yours,
isn't it? **is it?**

c) You have got a bike,
haven't you? have you?

d) They haven't got knives,
haven't they? **have they?**

EXERCICE 3

a) They are not my shoes, **are they**?

b) I haven't got the flu, **have I**?

c) All these stamps are yours, **aren't they**?

d) Karen is a teacher, **isn't she**?

e) We have not got twenty students, **have we**?

f) Brian is not sick, **is he**?

g) It is bad, **isn't it**?

h) You've got a great car, **haven't you**?

QUESTION-TAGS

To be

... am I?	*... am I not (*)?*
... are you?	*... aren't you?*
... is he?	*... isn't he?*
... is she?	*... isn't she?*
... is it?	*... isn't it?*
... are we?	*... aren't we?*
... are they?	*... aren't they?*

To have

... have I?	*... haven't I?*
... have you?	*... haven't you?*
... has he?	*... hasn't he?*
... has she?	*... hasn't she?*
... has it?	*... hasn't it?*
... have we?	*... haven't we?*
... have they?	*... haven't they?*

(* pas de forme contractée à la 1re personne du singulier.)

5 BE ET HAVE – QUESTION-TAGS

- **Emploi.**

Les *question-tags* (reprises interro-négatives) servent à confirmer une information.

- **Formation.**

Auxiliaire *be* ou *have* + pronom sujet.

- **La phrase est à la forme affirmative, le *tag* est négatif (forme contractée).**

You are Italian, aren't you?
She has got a brother, hasn't she?

- **La phrase est à la forme négative, le *tag* est à la forme affirmative.**

They are not married, are they?
We haven't got boots, have we?

1. Dis si dans les phrases suivantes, le *tag* doit être à la forme affirmative ou négative.

a) She is tall, ...?

forme ....

b) The baker hasn't got a daughter, ...?

forme ....

c) You aren't my friend, ...?

forme ....

d) Your cousins have got a CD player, ...?

forme ....

2. Souligne le *tag* qui te semble correct pour compléter la phrase.

a) He is your brother,
isn't he? is he?
b) This letter isn't yours,
isn't it? is it?
c) You have got a bike,
haven't you? have you?
d) They haven't got knives,
haven't they? have they?

3. Complète le *tag* à l'aide de l'auxiliaire *be* ou *have*.

a) They are not my shoes, ...
..............?

b) I haven't got the flu, ...
..............?

c) All these stamps are yours, ...
..............?

d) Karen is a teacher, ...?

e) We have not got twenty students,
..................................?

f) Brian is not sick, ...?

g) It is bad, ...?

h) You've got a great car,
..................................?

Voici un chapitre intéressant à découvrir... et utile à retenir!

EXERCICE 1

a) There **are** three bedrooms on the second floor.

b) In that house, there **are** two bathrooms.

c) There **is** a car in the garage.

d) Yes, there **is** a garden.

EXERCICE 2

a) four bedrooms
Are there four bedrooms in your house?

b) a cellar
Is there a cellar in your house?

c) an attic
Is there an attic in your house?

EXERCICE 3

a) is / kitchen / the / there / fridge / in / a / ?
Is there a fridge in the kitchen?

b) armchairs / four / are / in / there / living-room / the / .
There are four armchairs in the living-room.

c) the / windows / aren't / two / dining-room / there / in / .
There aren't two windows in the dining room.

6
THERE IS / THERE ARE

- **Pour dire « il y a ».**

– *There is* + nom singulier.
There is a garden.

– *There are* + nom pluriel.
There are flowers.

- **Questions.**

Is there? *Are there?*

Is there a cellar?
Are there any books?

- **Phrases négatives.**

There is not (isn't) ; there are not (aren't).

There isn't a fire-place.
There aren't any pictures on the wall.

- ***There + be* se conjugue à tous les temps.**

1. Complète les phrases à l'aide de *be* conjugué au présent, à la forme affirmative.

a) There .... three bedrooms on the second floor.

b) In that house, there .... two bathrooms.

c) There .... a car in the garage.

d) Yes, there .... a garden.

2. Demande à ton correspondant anglais ce qu'il y a dans sa maison. Utilise les mots proposés entre parenthèses.

Ex. : (balcony)
Is there a balcony in your house?

a) (four bedrooms)

....?

b) (a cellar)

....?

c) (an attic)

....?

3. Remets les mots dans le bon ordre pour faire des phrases correctes.

a) is / kitchen / the / there /fridge / in / a / ?

....

b) armchairs / four / are / in / there / living-room / the / .

....

....

c) the / windows / aren't / two / dining-room / there / in / .

....

....

EXERCICE 1

a) swimming / the / in / Jane / swimming-pool / is.
Jane is swimming in the swimming-pool.

b) raining / it / is / ?
Is it raining?

c) not / feeling /are / they / well / .
They are not feeling well.

EXERCICE 2

a) John is helping his mother.
John **is not helping** his mother.
(isn't helping)

b) We are watching a movie.
We **are not watching** a movie.
(aren't watching)

c) I am phoning Peter.
I **am not phoning** Peter.
(I'm not phoning)

EXERCICE 3

a) Is your father getting dressed?
Yes, **my father is getting dressed. (My father's getting dressed.)**

b) Are they fighting?
No, **they are not fighting. (They aren't fighting.)**

c) Is your friend working now?
Yes, **my friend is working now. (My friend's working now.)**

EXERCICE 4

a) **Are you cooking dinner?**
No, I am not cooking dinner.

b) **Is she pulling the cat's tail?**
No, she is not pulling the cat's tail.

c) **Are Bob and Martin studying at the moment?**
No, Bob and Martin are not studying at the moment.

FORMES CONTRACTÉES

Phrases affirmatives

I am - I'm
you are - you're
he is - he's
she is - she's
it is - it's
we are - we're
they are - they're
} *sleeping*

Phrases négatives

I am not - I'm not
you are not - you aren't
he is not - he isn't
she is not - she isn't
it is not - it isn't
we are not - we aren't
they are not - they aren't
} *working*

7 PRÉSENT PROGRESSIF (1)

● **Emploi.**

Le présent progressif ou continu sert à parler de ce que tu es en train de faire ou d'une action qui est en train de se passer.

I am leaving now.
Je m'en vais maintenant. / Je suis en train de m'en aller.

● **Construction.**

Sujet + *be* au présent + verbe en *-ing*.
I am learning English.

● **Questions.**

Be + sujet + verbe en *-ing*.
Is she taking a shower?

● **Phrases négatives.**

Sujet + *be* + *not* + verbe en *-ing*.
They are not listening to you.

1. Remets les mots dans le bon ordre pour former des phrases correctes.

a) swimming / the/ in / Jane / swimming-pool/ is / .

....

....

b) raining / it / is / ?

....

c) not / feeling / are / they / well / .

....

2. Mets ces phrases à la forme négative, puis indique entre parenthèses la forme contractée du groupe verbal.

Ex. : My grand children are writing a book.
My grand children are not writing a book. (aren't writing)

a) John is helping his mother.

....

b) We are watching a movie.

....

c) I am phoning Peter.

....

3. Réponds aux questions suivantes :

a) Is your father getting dressed?

Yes, ...

b) Are they fighting?

No, ...

c) Is your friend working now?

Yes, ...

4. Trouve les questions correspondant aux réponses suivantes.

a) ....

No, I am not cooking dinner.

b) ....

No, she is not pulling the cat's tail.

c) ....

No, Bob and Martin are not studying at the moment.

EXERCICE 1

a) Are you doing your homework?
Yes, **I am**.

b) Are they answering questions?
Yes, **they are**.

c) Is he listening to the news?
No, **he isn't**.

d) Are you complaining now?
No, **I'm not**.

e) Am I improving my English?
Yes, **you are**.

EXERCICE 2

a) Your grandfather isn't going to school, **is he**?

b) The phone is ringing, **isn't it**?

c) You are coming, **aren't you**?

d) They are not drinking alcohol, **are they**?

e) You are not hiding, **are you**?

EXERCICE 3

a) You are listening to me, are not you?
aren't you?

b) Are they all eating? Yes, they're.
they are.
(➜ La réponse courte ne se contracte pas à la forme affirmative.)

c) Is Bob phoning? No, he aren't.
he isn't.

d) The baby is not crying, 's he?
is he?

e) Her husband is travelling, he is not?
isn't he?

RÉPONSES COURTES
voir chapitre 4.

QUESTION-TAGS
voir chapitre 5.

8 PRÉSENT PROGRESSIF (2)

● **Réponses courtes :**
pour éviter de reprendre toute une phrase.

Pronom sujet + *be* (affirmatif ou négatif).
Is she teaching now?
Yes, she is. No, she isn't.

● ***Question-tags :***
pour demander à quelqu'un de confirmer une information.
« N'est-ce pas ? », « hein ? », « si ? ».

– **Phrase affirmative** :
be + *not* + pronom sujet.
Peter is sleeping, isn't he?

– **Phrase négative** :
be + pronom sujet.
You are not smoking, are you?

1. Donne des réponses courtes aux questions que l'on te pose.

a) Are you doing your homework?

Yes, ...

b) Are they answering questions?

Yes, ...

c) Is he listening to the news?

No, ...

d) Are you complaining now?

No, ...

e) Am I improving my English?

Yes, ...

2. Tu es curieux. Demande confirmation des informations suivantes.

a) Your grandfather isn't going to school, ...?

b) The phone is ringing, ...?

c) You are coming, ...?

d) They are not drinking alcohol, ...?

e) You are not hiding, ...?

3. Ton ami espagnol fait beaucoup d'erreurs en anglais. Corrige les erreurs dans les réponses courtes et *question-tags* soulignés.

a) You are listening to me, <u>are not you</u>?

....

b) Are they all eating? Yes, <u>they're</u>.

....

c) Is Bob phoning? No, <u>he aren't</u>.

....

d) The baby is not crying, <u>'s he</u>?

....

e) Her husband is travelling, <u>he is not</u>?

....

EXERCICE 1

Steward **wants** to leave now. He **looks** tired. I **know** Steward well. We **go** to school together and we **live** on the same street. When I **need** help with my homework, he always **helps** me.

→ *Attention, il ne faut pas oublier le* **s** *à la 3ᵉ personne du singulier.*

EXERCICE 2

a) Does Jane understand Russian?
No, Jane does not (doesn't) understand Russian.

b) Do you believe him?
No, I do not (don't) believe him.

c) Do they live together?
No, they do not (don't) live together.

d) Does he help you a lot?
No, he does not (doesn't) help me a lot.

EXERCICE 3

Demande à Larry

a) s'il aime le fromage ?
Do you like cheese?

b) si Charlotte le connaît ?
Does Charlotte know you?

EXERCICE 4

a) Do you wear jeans? No, I do not.
No, I **don't**.

b) Does she ride horses? No, she does not.
No, she **doesn't**.

c) Do they laugh very loud? No, they do not.
No, they **don't**.

TO DO

Formes contractées	**Réponses courtes**	**Question-tags**
I / you / we / they do not = I / you / we / they don't	*Yes, I / you / we / they do ; he / she / it does.*	*... do I / you / we / they ; does he / she / it?*
he / she / it does not = he / she / it doesn't	*No, I / you / we / they don't ; he / she / it doesn't.*	*...don't I / you / we / they ; doesn't he / she / it?*

***TO KNOW* AU PRÉSENT SIMPLE**

I know
you know
he / she / it knows
we know
they know

9 PRÉSENT SIMPLE

Emploi.

– On l'utilise avec les verbes d'action pour parler d'une action répétée ou d'une habitude dans le présent.
I go to school every day.

– On l'utilise avec les verbes d'état : *to understand, to know, to want, to like...*

Construction.

I like cats. *He like**s** cats.*

→ Attention au *s* à la 3e personne du singulier !

Questions.

Do / does + sujet + verbe à l'infinitif sans *to.*
Does she read?

Phrases négatives.

Sujet + *do not / does not* + verbe.
I do not know.

1. Complète le texte à l'aide des verbes entre parenthèses, conjugués au présent simple.

Steward .... (want) to leave now. He .... (look) tired. I .... (know) Steward well. We .... (go) to school together and we .... (live) on the same street. When I .... (need) help with my homework, he always .... (help) me.

2. Réponds aux questions à la forme négative, en faisant des phrases complètes.

a) Does Jane understand Russian?

....

b) Do you believe him?

....

c) Do they live together?

....

d) Does he help you a lot?

....

3. Comment demanderais-tu à Larry :

a) s'il aime le fromage ?

....

b) si Charlotte le connaît ?

....

4. Écris la forme contractée des réponses courtes soulignées.

a) Do you wear jeans? No, I <u>do not</u>.

....

b) Does she ride horses? No, she <u>does not</u>.

....

c) Do they laugh very loud?
No, they <u>do not</u>.

....

QUELQUES VERBES D'ÉTAT
to believe : croire
to enjoy : bien aimer
to hate : détester
to know : savoir
to like : aimer
to love : adorer
to understand : comprendre
to want : vouloir

EXERCICE 1

a) He **drinks** coffee every day.
(➜ Cette phrase est au présent simple car elle exprime l'habitude.)

b) What **do** they **want** to do?
(➜ want *est un verbe d'état.)*

c) Look at me! I **am flying!**
(➜ La phrase est au présent progressif car l'action est en train d'avoir lieu.)

d) Why **are** you **complaining** now?

EXERCICE 2

a) They don't understand you, **do they**?

b) Your cousin is helping you, **isn't he**?

c) You don't believe me, **do you**?

d) Philip is feeding the birds, **isn't he**?

EXERCICE 3

a) Do you like sports?
Yes, I do / No, I don't.

b) Do you watch TV every evening?
Yes, I do / No, I don't.

c) Are you sitting?
Yes, I am / No, I'm not.

d) Is it raining?
Yes, it is / No, it isn't.

e) Do you like this exercise?
Yes, I do / No, I don't.

f) Are you wearing trousers?
Yes, I am / No, I'm not.

10 PRÉSENT PROGRESSIF OU PRÉSENT SIMPLE ?

Présent progressif.

Il s'utilise :
– avec les verbes d'action ;
– pour décrire ce qui est en train de se passer.

Présent simple.

Il s'utilise :
– avec les verbes d'état ;
– pour parler de ce que tu fais habituellement.

Réponses courtes.

– Avec le présent progressif :
Yes, I am ; no, she isn't.
– Avec le présent simple :
Yes I do ; no, he doesn't.

Question-tags.

– Avec le présent progressif :
am I? ; isn't she?
– Avec le présent simple :
do I? ; doesn't he?

1. Conjugue les verbes entre parenthèses au présent progressif ou au présent simple selon ce qui est nécessaire.

a) He .... (drink) coffee every day.

b) What .... (do) they ....
.... (want) to do?

c) Look at me! I .... (fly)!

d) Why .... (be) you
.... (complain) now?

2. Complète les phrases avec le bon *question-tag*.

a) They don't understand you, ...
.....................?

b) Your cousin is helping you, ...
.....................?

c) You don't believe me, ...?

d) Philip is feeding the birds, ...
.................?

3. Le jeu de la vérité ! Apporte à ces six questions des réponses courtes. Attention, tu n'as que deux minutes pour faire cet exercice !

a) Do you like sports?

....

b) Do you watch TV every evening?

....

c) Are you sitting?

....

d) Is it raining?

....

e) Do you like this exercise?

....

f) Are you wearing trousers?

....

Simple ou progressif,
conjugue toujours au présent
le verbe « se motiver » !

EXERCICE 1

a) Shakespeare **was** a play-writer.

b) Where **were** you born?`
(➜ *En anglais, « Je suis né » se traduit avec l'auxiliaire* be *au prétérit :* I was born*)*

c) My shoes **were not (weren't)** here this morning.

e) Why **was** she angry?

f) Yesterday, we **were** in Switzerland.

EXERCICE 2

a) Were the bottles full?
No, **they weren't**.

b) Was the car in the garage?
Yes, **it was**.

c) Were your slippers under the bed?
Yes, **they were**.

d) Was Helen born in South Africa?
No, **she wasn't**.

e) Were the horses wild?
Yes, **they were**.

EXERCICE 3

a) Sarah wasn't at the hotel, **was she**?

b) The zoo-keepers were on holiday, **weren't they**?

c) You weren't in danger, **were you**?

d) I was silly, **wasn't I**?

EXERCICE 4

Demande à Jennifer

a) si elle était en Écosse, l'année dernière.
Were you in Scotland last year?

b) si son frère était avec elle.
Was your brother with you?

c) si les écossais étaient gentils.
Were Scottish people nice?

RÉPONSES COURTES

Yes, I was	*No, I wasn't*
you were	*you weren't*
he was	*he wasn't*
she was	*she wasn't*
it was	*it wasn't*
we were	*we weren't*
they were	*they weren't*

QUESTION-TAGS

... was I?	*... wasn't I?*
were you?	*weren't you?*
was he?	*wasn't he?*
was she?	*wasn't she?*
was it?	*wasn't it?*
were we?	*weren't we?*
were they?	*weren't they?*

FORMES CONTRACTÉES

Was et *were* ne se contractent qu'à la forme négative !

was not	*were not*
= wasn't	*= weren't*

11 WAS / WERE

Le prétérit est un temps du passé.

- ***Be* au prétérit.**

I / he / she / it was ;
we / you / they were.

- **Questions.**

Was I / he / she / it ;
were we / you / they?

- **Phrases négatives.**

No, I / he / she / it was not ;
you / we / they were not.
was not = wasn't
were not = weren't

- **Réponses courtes.**

Were you lonely?
Yes, I was ; no I was not (wasn't).

- ***Question-tags.***

She wasn't happy, was she?
They were cold, weren't they?

1. Complète les phrases à l'aide de *was* ou *were*, à la forme affirmative, interrogative ou négative.

a) Shakespeare .... a play-writer.

b) Where .... you born?

c) My shoes .... (not) here this morning.

d) Why .... she angry?

e) Yesterday, we .... in Switzerland.

2. Réponds aux questions par des réponses courtes.

a) Were the bottles full?

No, ...

b) Was the car in the garage?

Yes, ...

c) Were your slippers under the bed?

Yes, ...

d) Was Helen born in South Africa?

No, ...

e) Were the horses wild?

Yes, ...

3. Complète les phrases par le *tag* qui convient.

a) Sarah wasn't at the hotel, ...

............?

b) The zoo-keepers were on

holiday, ...?

c) You weren't in danger, ...?

d) I was silly, ...?

4. Demande à Jennifer :

a) si elle était en Écosse, l'année dernière.

....

....?

b) si son frère était avec elle.

....?

c) si les Écossais étaient gentils.

....?

EXERCICE 1

a) The firemen / have / a lot of work / .
The firemen had a lot of work.

b) This child / have / bad marks / ?
Did this child have bad marks?

c) We / not have / a good time / .
We did not (didn't) have a good time.

EXERCICE 2

a) Did Jane and Paddy have books to read?
No, **they didn't**.

b) Did you have good weather?
Yes, **I / we did**.

c) Did she have a red hat?
No, **she didn't**.

EXERCICE 3

a) Ted had a great parrot, **didn't he**?

b) All the children had breakfast, **didn't they**?

c) Mary didn't have the right map, **did she**?

d) Your aunt had a cold, **didn't she**?

EXERCICE 4

a) Tu n'avais pas de téléphone, si ?
You didn't have a phone, did you?

b) Est-ce que Keith avait un appartement ?
Did Keith have a flat?

c) Nous avions une voiture, n'est-ce-pas ?
We had a car, didn't we?

Rappel
Au prétérit, l'auxiliaire *do* devient *did* à toutes les personnes.

12 *HAD*

Have est un auxiliaire mais au prétérit, il se construit comme un verbe ordinaire.

● **Construction.**

Had à toutes les personnes.

À toutes les personnes, on utilise ***did*** pour les :

● **questions.**

Did you have a good holiday?

● **phrases négatives.**

They did not have a map.

● **réponses courtes.**

Did you have a good trip? Yes, I did. No, I did not (didn't).

● **phrases interro-négatives.**

... She had a great time, didn't she?

1. Compose des phrases à l'aide des mots. Conjuge *have* au prétérit.

Attention, certaines phrases sont à la forme interrogative !

a) The firemen / have / a lot of work / .

....

b) This child / have / bad marks / ?

....

c) We / not have / a good time / .

....

2. Réponds aux questions à l'aide de réponses courtes.

a) Did Jane and Paddy have books to read?

No, ...

b) Did you have good weather?

Yes, ...

c) Did she have a red hat?

No, ...

3. Complète les phrases interro-négatives.

a) Ted had a great parrot,

....?

b) All the children had breakfast,

....?

c) Mary didn't have the right map,

....?

d) Your aunt had a cold,

....?

4. Comment dirais-tu en anglais :

a) Tu n'avais pas de téléphone, si ?

....

b) Est-ce que Keith avait un appartement ?

....

c) Nous avions une voiture, n'est-ce-pas ?

....

EXERCICE 1

a) To feel **irrégulier** **felt**
b) To clean **régulier** **cleaned**
c) To forget **irrégulier** **forgot**
d) To give **irrégulier** **gave**

EXERCICE 2

Mr Beaver **arrived** early in London. He **went** straight to the bank, and **met** the manager. The manager **did not (didn't) want** to listen to him. Mr Beaver **got** angry.

EXERCICE 3

a) You went to the wrong building.
I **did not (didn't) go to the wrong building**.

b) The dog didnt' catch the ball.
The dog **caught the ball**.

c) They ate lunch.
They **did not (didn't) eat lunch**.

EXEMPLES DE PRÉTÉRITS RÉGULIERS

to arrive	*arrived*	arriver
to clean	*cleaned*	nettoyer
to enjoy	*enjoyed*	apprécier, bien aimer
to kick	*kicked*	donner un coup de pied
to laugh	*laughed*	rire
to love	*loved*	aimer, adorer
to phone	*phoned*	téléphoner
to play	*played*	jouer
to start	*started*	commencer
to want	*wanted*	vouloir

Pour les **prétérits irréguliers**, reporte-toi à l'Annexe n°1.

EXERCICE 4

a) What **did James sweep**?
James swept the kitchen floor.

b) What **did they do**?
They laughed.

c) Who **did you phone**?
I phoned my sister.

d) What time **did they start**?
They started at 9 AM.

13 PRÉTÉRIT SIMPLE (1)

● **Forme affirmative.**

– Verbes réguliers.
On ajoute *-ed*, au radical du verbe.
*I play**ed** darts.*

– Verbes irréguliers.
(Voir Annexe n° 1).

● **Questions et phrases négatives.**

Elles se construisent avec l'auxiliaire *do* au prétérit : *did* à toutes les personnes. La forme est identique pour les verbes réguliers et irréguliers.

– *Did* + sujet + verbe à l'infinitif sans *to*.
Did you enjoy it?

– Sujet + *did not* + verbe à l'infinitif sans *to*.
She did not get up early.

1. Les verbes suivants sont-ils réguliers ou irréguliers ? Écris leur prétérit.

a) To feel

....

b) To clean

....

c) To forget

....

d) To give

....

2. Complète les phrases. Conjugue les verbes entre parenthèses au prétérit simple, à la forme affirmative ou négative.

Mr Beaver .... (arrive) early in London. He .... (go) straight to the bank, and .... (meet) the manager. The manager .... (not want) to listen to him. Mr Beaver .... (get) angry.

3. Exprime le contraire.

a) You went to the wrong building.
I ....

b) The dog didn't catch the ball.
The dog ....

c) They ate lunch.
They ....

4. Trouve les questions qui correspondent aux mots soulignés.

a) What ....?
James swept the kitchen floor.

b) What ....?
They laughed.

c) Who ....?
I phoned my sister.

d) What time ....?
They started at 9 AM.

La forme contractée de *did not* est *didn't*.

EXERCICE 1

L'été dernier, Peter a passé trois semaines en Australie. Il est allé à la plage et il a nagé dans la mer. Il a vu des kangourous mais il n'a pas pris de photos.

Last summer, Peter spent three weeks in Australia. He went to the beach and he swam in the sea. He saw kangaroos but he didn't take photographs.

EXERCICE 2

a) you / your / last / grandmother / did / month / visit / ?
Did you visit your grandmother last month? *ou* **Did your grandmother visit you last month?**

b) big / a / smoked / last / cigar / father / night / my / .
My father smoked a big cigar last night.

c) London / plane / in / didn't / the / land / .
The plane didn't land in London.

EXERCICE 3

a) When did the travel agency open? (two weeks)
The travel agency opened two weeks ago.

b) When did you fly to New York? (three days)
I flew to New York three days ago.

c) When did they deliver this parcel? (ten minutes)
They delivered this parcel ten minutes ago.

QUELQUES MARQUEURS DE TEMPS

yesterday : hier
the day before yesterday : avant-hier
last night : la nuit dernière
last week : la semaine dernière
last month : le mois dernier
last year : l'année dernière
one hour ago : il y a une heure
two days ago : il y a deux jours
three months ago : il y a trois mois
four years ago : il y a quatre ans

14 PRÉTÉRIT SIMPLE (2)

- **Le prétérit ou *simple past*.**

On l'ulilise pour relater des événements totalement passés.
We walked home and watched a movie on TV.

- **Les marqueurs de temps.**

Yesterday, last week, last year... accompagnent souvent une phrase au prétérit et se placent en fin de phrase.
Did you have a good time yesterday?

- **Pour dire « il y a deux mois » :**

phrase au prétérit + expression de temps + ***ago*** en fin de phrase.
I met him two months ago.

1. Raconte l'histoire en anglais.

L'été dernier, Peter a passé trois semaines en Australie. Il est allé à la plage et il a nagé dans la mer. Il a vu des kangourous mais il n'a pas pris de photos.

....

....

....

....

....

2. Remets les mots dans le bon ordre pour faire des phrases correctes.

a) you / your / last / grandmother / did / month / visit / ?

....

....

b) big / a / smoked / last / cigar / father / night / my / .

....

....

c) London / plane / in / didn't / the / land / .

....

....

3. Réponds aux questions à l'aide des mots entre parenthèses + *ago*.

Ex. : When did Jane and Chris leave the house? (two hours)
Jane and Chris left the house two hours ago.

a) When did the travel agency open? (two weeks)

....

....

b) When did you fly to New York? (three days)

....

....

c) When did they deliver this parcel? (ten minutes)

....

....

EXERCICE 1

a) The dog jumped on you, didn't it?
prétérit simple

b) She draws butterflies, doesn't she?
présent simple

c) You didn't phone your father, did you?
prétérit simple

d) You like running, don't you?
présent simple

EXERCICE 2

a) Do you make your bed every day?
Yes, I do / No, I don't.

b) Did you brush your teeth last night?
Yes, I did / No, I didn't.

c) Did you eat meat yesterday?
Yes, I did / No, I didn't.

d) Did the telephone ring five minutes ago?
Yes, it did / No, it didn't.

e) Does your mother cook dinner?
Yes, she does / No, she doesn't.

EXERCICE 3

a) **Your mother picks up the phone, doesn't she?**
Yes, my mother picks up the phone.

b) **They drew a picture, didn't they?**
Yes, they drew a picture.

c) **Your sister and your brother always fight, don't they?**
Yes, my sister and my brother always fight.

RÉPONSES COURTES	**phrase affirmative**	**phrase négative**
Présent simple	*Yes, I / you / we / they do* *Yes, he / she / it does*	*No, I / you / we / they don't* *No, he / she / it doesn't*
Prétérit simple	*Yes, I / you / he / she / it / we / they did*	*No, I / you / he / she / it / we / they didn't*
QUESTION-TAGS		
Présent simple	*..., do I / you / we / they?* *..., does he / she / it ?*	*..., don't I / you / we / they?* *..., doesn't he / she / it ?*
Prétérit simple	*..., did I / you / he / she / it / we / they?*	*..., didn't I / you / he / she / it / we / they?*

Répondre à des questions, c'est toujours intéressant : ça te permet d'apprendre de nouvelles choses.

15 RÉPONSES COURTES ET *TAGS*

On utilise ***do / does*** pour le présent simple, ***did*** pour le prétérit simple.

- **Réponses courtes.**

– *Yes,* ***I do.***
No, ***we don't.***
– *Yes,* ***he does.***
No, ***she doesn't****.*
– *Yes,* ***we did****.*
No, ***it didn't****.*

- ***Question-tags.***

– ..., do you?
..., don't you?
You don't swim, do you?
You work, don't you?
– ..., does he?
..., doesn't he?
He doesn't care, does he?
He understands, doesn't he?
– ..., did she?
..., didn't we?
She didn't stop, did she?
We left, didn't we?

1. Les phrases suivantes sont-elles au présent simple ou au prétérit simple ?

a) The dog jumped on you, didn't it?

....

b) She draws butterflies, doesn't she?

....

c) You didn't phone your father, did you?

....

d) You like running, don't you?

....

2. Apporte aux questions des réponses courtes. Donne celles qui te concernent.

a) Do you make your bed every day?

....

b) Did you brush your teeth last night?

....

c) Did you eat meat yesterday?

....

d) Did the telephone ring five minutes ago?

....

e) Does your mother cook dinner?

....

3. Trouve les questions en utilisant une réponse interro-négative *(tag)*, comme dans l'exemple.

Ex. : ***You queued at the butcher's, didn't you?***
Yes, I queued at the butcher's.

a) ....?
Yes, my mother picks up the phone.

b) ....?
Yes, they drew a picture.

c) ....?
Yes, my sister and my brother always fight.

EXERCICE 1

a) <u>Was</u> they sitting or standing?
Were they sitting or standing?

b) She <u>is</u> hurting her sister.
She **was** hurting her sister.
(➜ She is hurting *est le présent progressif.)*

c) Why were you <u>phoned</u> him?
Why were you **phoning** him?
(➜ Le prétérit progressif se forme avec l'auxiliaire be *au prétérit + verbe en* -ing.*)*

d) <u>I's</u> not smoking.
I **was** not **(wasn't)** smoking.
(➜ La forme contractée de was not *est* wasn't.*)*

e) Mark was always <u>fight</u> with his friends.
Mark was always **fighting** with his friends.

EXERCICE 2

a) **Were** you **sleeping**?

b) No, Nancy **was not (wasn't) helping** me.

c) Thank you! I **was waiting** for it.

d) **Were** they **speaking** slowly?

e) Sorry, I **was not (wasn't) listening!**

EXERCICE 3

a) To sleep : **I was sleeping / I wasn't sleeping.**

b) To eat dinner : **I was eating dinner / I wasn't eating dinner.**

c) To watch TV : **I was watching TV / I wasn't watching TV.**

d) To do your homework : **I was doing my homework / I wasn't doing my homework.**

e) To study English : **I was studying English / I wasn't studying English.**

FORMES CONTRACTÉES

I was not running	*I wasn't running*
You were not cooking	*You weren't cooking*
He was not cleaning	*He wasn't cleaning*
She was not flying	*She wasn't flying*
It was not working	*It wasn't working*
We were not building	*We weren't building*
They were not parking	*They weren't parking*

➜ Au prétérit progressif, seule la forme négative se contracte !

16 PRÉTÉRIT PROGRESSIF

● **Emploi.**

Le prétérit progressif sert à décrire une action qui s'est prolongée dans le passé. Il correspond à l'imparfait en français.

Yesterday, at this time, I was travelling.

Hier, au même moment, j'étais en train de voyager.

● **Construction.**

Sujet + *be* au prétérit + verbe en *-ing*.

She was taking a shower.

● **Questions.**

Be au prétérit + sujet + verbe en *-ing*.

Were you leaving?

● **Phrases négatives.**

Sujet + *be* au prétérit + *not* + verbe en *-ing*.

They were not (weren't) complaining.

1. Dans chaque phrase, le groupe verbal au prétérit progressif comporte une erreur. Souligne-la et corrige-la.

Ex. : Mary ***did*** *not sleeping at 9 PM.*
Mary ***was*** *not sleeping at 9 PM.*

a) Was they sitting or standing?

....

b) She is hurting her sister.

....

c) Why were you phoned him?

....

d) I's not smoking.

....

e) Mark was always fight with his friends.

....

2. Conjugue les verbes entre parenthèses au prétérit progressif.

a) .... you .... (sleep)?

b) No, Nancy .... (not help) me.

c) Thank you! I .... (wait) for it.

d) .... they .... (speak) slowly?

e) Sorry, I .... (not listen)!

3. Dis ce que tu faisais ou ne faisais pas, hier soir à 19 h. Compose des phrases à l'aide des verbes proposés.

a) To sleep : ....

....

b) To eat dinner : ....

....

c) To watch TV : ....

....

d) To do your homework : ....

....

e) To study English : ....

....

EXERCICE 1

a) *The radio was working* est une phrase au prétérit progressif.
Vrai

b) *I was sleeping when she opened the door* signifie « J'ai dormi quand elle a ouvert la porte ».
Faux
(➜ Cette phrase signifie « J'étais en train de dormir lorsqu'elle a ouvert la porte ». Was sleeping *est au prétérit progressif ; il se traduit par un imparfait en français « je dormais » ou « j'étais en train de dormir ».* Opened *est au prétérit simple; il se traduit par un passé composé en français « elle a ouvert ».)*

EXERCICE 2

a) Manfred **was resting** when he heard the news.

b) **Were** you **driving** when the storm started?

c) When I met Tom, he **was not having** fun.

EXERCICE 3

a) The plane **was landing** when the captain **started** to speak to the passengers.

b) We **were cooking** when she **told** us the news.

c) I **was enjoying** myself when suddenly, the music **stopped**.

d) Yes, John **was queueing** when he **saw** Jennie.

17 PRÉTÉRIT PROGRESSIF ET PRÉTÉRIT SIMPLE

● **Le prétérit progressif est souvent employé avec le prétérit simple.**

Last night, I was sleeping. Suddenly, I heard a noise.
La nuit dernière, j'étais en train de dormir. Soudain, j'ai entendu un bruit.

● **Le prétérit progressif.**

Il insiste sur la durée d'une action dans le passé : «J'étais en train de dormir. »

● **Le prétérit simple.**

Il décrit une action brève dans le passé : « J'ai entendu. »

1. Ces affirmations sont-elles vraies ou fausses ?

a) The radio was working est une phrase au prétérit progressif.

....

b) I was sleeping when she opened the door signifie « J'ai dormi quand elle a ouvert la porte. »

....

2. Conjugue les verbes entre parenthèses au prétérit progressif.

a) Manfred .... (rest) when he heard the news.

b) .... you .... (drive) when the storm started?

c) When I met Tom, he ....

.... (not have) fun.

3. Conjugue les verbes entre parenthèses au prétérit simple ou au prétérit progressif.

a) The plane .... (land) when the captain .... (start) to speak to the passengers.

b) We .... (cook) when she .... (tell) us the news.

c) I .... (enjoy) myself when suddenly the music .... (stop).

d) Yes, John .... (queue) when he .... (see) Jennie.

> Le prétérit progressif et le prétérit simple apparaissent souvent dans la même phrase avec ***when***.
> *Ex. : They were working when the bell rang.*
> Le prétérit simple apparaît dans la proposition introduite par ***when***.

EXERCICE 1

a) To cut **cut**
b) To hide **hidden**
c) To hold **held**
d) To keep **kept**
e) To spend **spent**
f) To stand **stood**
g) To know **known**
h) To feel **felt**
i) To do **done**

EXERCICE 2

a) the / paid / not / has / Jean / bill / .
Jean has not paid the bill.

b) you / your / lesson / have / learnt / ?
Have you learnt your lesson?

c) has / locked / the / Paul / door / .
Paul has locked the door.

EXERCICE 3

a) **Has Jane cooked dinner?**
No, Jane has not cooked dinner.

b) **Have you forgotten your keys?**
Yes, I have forgotten my keys.

c) **Has she hurt him?**
Yes, she has hurt him.

d) **Have you / we corrected your / our homework?**
No, we have not corrected our homework.

LES PARTICIPES PASSÉS

Réguliers : on ajoute ***-ed*** au radical du verbe.

Ex. : played, worked, jumped...

Irréguliers : il faut les apprendre par cœur ! (Voir Annexe n°1.)

EXERCICE 4

a) They have lost their minds!
They've lost their minds!

b) Sue has not guessed!
Sue hasn't guessed!

c) Yes, I have read this novel.
Yes, I've read this novel.

18 *PRESENT PERFECT* (1)

Le *present perfect* est un temps du présent.

- **Construction.**

Sujet + *have / has*
+ participe passé du verbe
He has bought new shoes.
Il a acheté de nouvelles chaussures.

- **Questions.**

Have / has + sujet
+ participe passé
Have you seen him?

- **Phrases négatives.**

Sujet + *have / has* + *not*
+ participe passé

- **Au *present perfect, have* est un auxiliaire.**

Il se contracte (voir chapitre 4).

1. Trouve le participe passé de ces verbes irréguliers.

a) To cut ....

b) To hide ....

c) To hold ....

d) To keep ....

e) To spend ....

f) To stand ....

g) To know ....

h) To feel ....

i) To do ....

2. Mets les mots dans le bon ordre pour faire des phrases correctes.

Attention, certaines phrases sont des questions !

a) the / paid / not / has / Jean / bill / .

....

b) you / your / lesson / have / learnt / ?

....

c) has / locked / the / Paul /door / .

....

3. Trouve les questions à ces réponses.

a) ....?
No, Jane has not cooked dinner.

b) ....?
Yes, I have forgotten my keys.

c) ....?
Yes, she has hurt him.

d) ....?
No, we have not corrected our homework.

4. Écris la forme contractée des verbes.

a) They have lost their minds!

....

b) Sue has not guessed!

....

c) Yes, I have read this novel.

....

EXERCICE 1

a) Le bébé avait faim. Dis que tu l'as nourri. (feed)
I have fed the baby.

b) Eva ne voulait plus prendre le bus. Dis qu'elle a acheté une voiture. (buy)
Eva has bought a car.

c) La maison était sale. Dis que tu l'as nettoyée. (clean)
I have cleaned the house.

EXERCICE 2

a) Has the mailman left?
Yes, the mailman has just left.

b) Have you had lunch?
Yes, I have just had lunch.

c) Has Erick spoken to the headmaster?
Yes, Erick has just spoken to the headmaster.

EXERCICE 3

a) John has just finished his homework.

1. John vient juste de finir ses devoirs.

2. John va juste finir ses devoirs.

3. John finit simplement ses devoirs.

(➜ Just + present perfect *indique qu'une action vient juste de se terminer.)*

b) Mary has not seen this movie.

1. Mary ne veut pas voir ce film.

2. Mary n'a pas vu ce film.

3. Mary n'a jamais vu ce film.

19 *PRESENT PERFECT* (2)

● **Emploi.**

Le *present perfect* indique le résultat d'une action.
She has broken her leg.
= aujourd'hui, elle a la jambe cassée.

● **Avec *just* à la forme affirmative :**

il indique qu'une action passée vient juste de se terminer.
We have just phoned him.
Nous venons juste de l'appeler au téléphone.

Have you heard from him lately?
Yes, I have just talked to him.

1. En utilisant les verbes entre parenthèses, fais des phrases pour indiquer le résultat des actions suivantes.

a) Le bébé avait faim. Dis que tu l'as nourri. (feed)

....

b) Eva ne voulait plus prendre le bus. Dis qu'elle a acheté une voiture. (buy)

....

c) La maison était sale. Dis que tu l'as nettoyée. (clean)

....

2. Réponds aux questions en faisant des phrases avec *just*.

a) Has the mailman left?

Yes, ...

b) Have you had lunch?

Yes, ...

c) Has Erick spoken to the head-master?

Yes, ...

3. Que signifient les phrases suivantes ?
Souligne la bonne traduction.

a) John has just finished his homework.
1. Jonh vient juste de finir ses devoirs.
2. John va juste finir ses devoirs.
3. John finit simplement ses devoirs.

b) Mary has not seen this movie.
1. Mary ne veut pas voir ce film.
2. Mary n'a pas vu ce film.
3. Mary n'a jamais vu ce film.

EXERCICE 1

a) **When** did they arrive?

b) **How long** have the windows been closed?

c) I've **just** had a conversation with Paul.

d) Sophie came back two weeks **ago**.

EXERCICE 2

a) Last month, I **bought** a train ticket and **took** the ferry to Dover.

b) How long **has** she **ignored** you?

c) Yes, I **saw** Thomas three weeks ago.

d) When **did** you **decide** to write this book?

e) No, I'm not sleepy. I **have** just **had** a nap.

EXERCICE 3

a) You haven't answered me!
Tu ne m'as pas répondu !

b) When did you burn this letter?
Quand as-tu brûlé cette lettre ?

c) They have just bought a new house!
Ils viennent juste d'acheter une nouvelle maison !

d) My cat saw a butterfly and he caught it.
Mon chat a vu un papillon et il l'a attrapé.

Remarque

Le **prétérit simple** et le ***present perfect*** se traduisent tous les deux par le passé composé en français.

À l'écrit, on peut aussi traduire le prétérit simple par le passé simple en français.

Ex. : They saw a horse.
Ils virent un cheval.

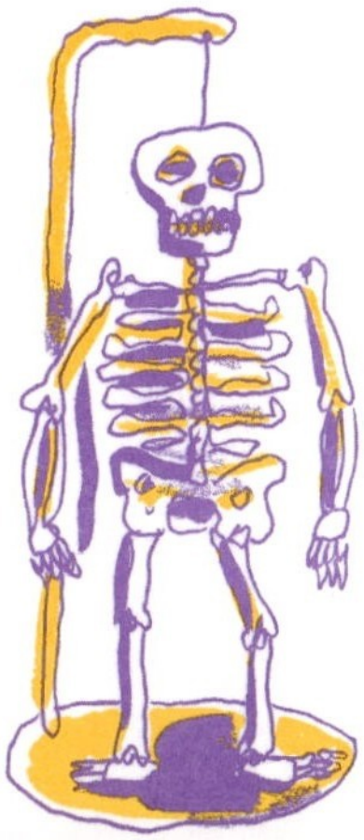

20 PRÉTÉRIT SIMPLE OU *PRESENT PERFECT* ?

● **Le prétérit simple.**

Il sert à raconter des événements passés.
We had a picnic and rode our bikes.

– ***When?*** pour poser une question.
When did you meet her?

– ***Ago*** pour répondre.
Two weeks ago.

● **Le *present perfect*.**

Il sert à indiquer le résultat d'une action passée sur le présent.
They have cleaned the house.

– Avec ***just*** (voir chapitre 19).
She has just had lunch.

– ***How long?*** pour poser une question.
How long have you known this?

1. Complète les phrases à l'aide de *how long, when, ago* ou *just*.

a) .... did they arrive?

b) .... have the windows been closed?

c) I've .... had a conversation with Paul.

d) Sophie came back two weeks

....

2. Complète les phrases à l'aide des verbes entre parenthèses. Conjugue-les au prétérit simple ou au *present perfect*.

a) Last month, I .... (buy) a train ticket and .... (take) the ferry to Dover.

b) How long .... she .... (ignore) you?

c) Yes, I .... (see) Thomas three weeks ago.

d) When .... you .... (decide) to write this book?

e) No, I'm not sleepy. I .... just .... (have) a nap.

3. Comment traduirais-tu ces phrases en français ?

a) You haven't answered me!

....

b) When did you burn this letter?

....

c) They have just bought a new house!

....

....

d) My cat saw a butterfly and he caught it.

....

....

EXERCICE 1

a) Next week, I'm meeting Neil.
futur

b) No, I'm not listening to the news, now.
présent

c) Look, Uncle Jack is coming!
présent

> **Remarque**
> Le **présent progressif à valeur de futur se traduit par un présent simple** en français.
> *Ex. : Next week, she is not working.*
> La semaine prochaine, elle ne travaille pas.

EXERCICE 2

a) Demain, il prend l'avion pour l'Australie.

1. Tomorrow, he leaves for Australia.
2. Tomorrow, he left for Australia.
3. **Tomorrow, he is leaving for Australia.**

b) Ce soir, je vais au lit à 21 heures.

1. Next evening, I'm going to bed at 9 PM.
2. This night, I'm going to bed at 9 PM.
3. **This evening, I'm going to bed at 9 PM.**

c) L'année prochaine nous déménageons.

1. Next year, we are moved.
2. Next year, we have moved.
3. **Next year, we are moving.**

EXERCICE 3

Tomorrow, I'm getting up early *ou* **Tomorrow, I'm not getting up early.**

21

FUTUR – PRÉSENT PROGRESSIF

- **Le présent progressif a parfois un sens de futur.**

Il sert à parler des choses que tu as déjà planifiées.
When are you leaving?
I'm leaving tonight.
Quand pars-tu ?
Je pars ce soir.

- **Il est accompagné de marqueurs de temps futurs.**

tonight : this evening
tomorrow : demain
next week / next month / next year : la semaine prochaine, le mois prochain, l'année prochaine.

- **Construction.**

Voir chapitre 10.

1. Dans les phrases suivantes, le présent progressif a-t'il une valeur de présent ou de futur ?

a) Next week, I'm meeting Neil.

....

b) No, I'm not listening to the news, now.

....

c) Look, Uncle Jack is coming!

....

2. Souligne la bonne traduction des phrases suivantes.

a) Demain, il prend l'avion pour l'Australie.
1. Tomorrow, he leaves for Australia.
2. Tomorrow, he left for Australia.
3. Tomorrow, he is leaving for Australia.

b) Ce soir, je vais au lit à 21 heures.
1. Next evening, I'm going to bed at 9 PM.
2. This night, I'm going to bed at 9 PM.
3. This evening, I'm going to bed at 9 PM.

c) L'année prochaine nous déménageons.
1. Next year, we are moved.
2. Next year, we have moved.
3. Next year, we are moving.

3. Compose une phrase. Dis si tu as prévu ou non de te lever tôt demain.

....

....

....

....

Tu réussiras ces exercices
en un quart d'heure,
si tu te concentres bien...
Prêt(e) ?

EXERCICE 1

a) Tonight Neil is staying here.
Tonight, Neil is going to stay here.

b) I'm leaving soon.
I am going (I'm going) to leave soon.

c) You are not eating out tonight.
You are not going (aren't going) to eat out tonight.

d) No, we are not helping them.
No, we are not going (aren't going) to help them.

EXERCICE 2

a) **Is Barry going to arrive on time?**
No, Barry isn't going to arrive on time.

b) **Are my parents going to feed the turtle?**
Yes, your parents are going to feed the turtle.

c) **Is it going to be too late?**
No, it's not going to be too late.

EXERCICE 3

a) They're going to be angry.
They are going to be angry.

b) I'm not going to get dressed.
I am not going to get dressed.

c) We aren't going to phone.
We are not going to phone.

d) Paul's going to throw it away.
Paul is going to throw it away.

EXERCICE 4

I am going (I'm going) to become a teacher *ou* **I am not (I'm not) going to become a teacher.**

FORMES CONTRACTÉES

phrases affirmatives	*I am going to*	*I'm going to*
	You are going to	*You're going to*
	He is going to	*He's going to*
	She is going to	*She's going to*
	It is going to	*It's going to*
	We are going to	*We're going to*
	They are going to	*They're going to*
phrases négatives	*I am not going to*	*I'm not going to*
	You are not going to	*You aren't going to*
	He is not going to	*He isn't going to*
	She is not going to	*She isn't going to*
	It is not going to	*It isn't going to*
	We are not going to	*We aren't going to*
	They are not going to	*They aren't going to*

22 FUTUR – *GOING TO...*

● **Emploi.**

Le futur avec *going to* sert à parler des choses que tu as l'intention de faire.
I'm going to tell you a story.
Je vais te raconter une histoire.

● **Construction.**

Sujet + *be* au présent + *going to* + verbe à l'infinitif sans *to.*
My sister is going to study literature.

● **Questions.**

Be + sujet + *going to* + verbe.
Is she going to rent a flat?

● **Phrases négatives.**

Sujet + *be* + *not* + *going to* + verbe.
No, she is not going to leave.

1. Transforme les phrases au présent progressif en futur avec *going to*.

Ex. : Mom is giving me her watch.
Mom is going to give me her watch.

a) Tonight Neil is staying here.

....

b) I'm leaving soon.

....

c) You are not eating out tonight.

....

d) No, we are not helping them.

....

2. Trouve les questions à ces réponses.

a) ....?
No, Barry isn't going to arrive on time.

b) ....?
Yes, your parents are going to feed the turtle.

c) ....?
No, it's not going to be too late.

3. Reécris les phrases suivantes sans mettre les verbes à la forme contractée.

Ex. : She isn't going to like it.
She is not going to like it.

a) They're going to be angry.

....

b) I'm not going to get dressed.

....

c) We aren't going to phone.

....

d) Paul's going to throw it away.

....

4. Compose une phrase. Dis si tu as l'intention ou non de devenir professeur.

....

....

....

....

EXERCICE 1

a) invite / you / me / party / to / your / will / ?
Will you invite me to your party?

b) this / boys / you / not / the / ask / question / will / .
The boys will not ask you this question.

c) end / movie / will / soon / the / .
The movie will end soon.

EXERCICE 2

a) Will your friends agree with you?
No, my friends will not (won't) agree with me.

b) Will the fire burn all night long?
No, the fire will not (won't) burn all night long.

c) Will Paul wear his new suit?
No, Paul will not (won't) wear his new suit.

EXERCICE 3

Dis que :

a) tu apprendras tes leçons.
I will learn my lessons.

b tu ne regarderas pas la télévision tous les jours.
I will not (won't) watch television every day.

c) tu diras toujours la vérité.
I will always tell the truth.

EXERCICE 4

a) We will not work together again.
We won't work together again.

b) She will be scared.
She'll be scared.

c) I will help you tomorrow.
I'll help you tomorrow.

d) Bobby will not guess!
Bobby won't guess!

23 FUTUR SIMPLE – *WILL*

● **Emploi.**

Le futur simple sert à évoquer ce qui va se passer dans un avenir plus ou moins proche.

● **Construction.**

On utilise l'auxiliaire *will* à toutes les personnes.
Sujet + auxiliaire *will* + verbe à l'infinitif sans *to*
He will arrive on time.

● **Questions.**

Will + sujet + verbe
Will you dance with me?

● **Phrases négatives.**

Sujet + *will* + *not* + verbe
They will not listen to you.

● **Formes contractées.**

Ce sont les mêmes à toutes les personnes.
You will = you'll
She will not = she won't

1. Remets les mots dans le bon ordre pour faire des phrases correctes.

a) invite / you / me / party / your / to / will / ?

....

....

b) this / boys / you / not / the / ask / question / will / .

....

....

c) end / movie / will / soon / the / .

....

2. Réponds aux questions en faisant des phrases négatives.

a) Will your friends agree with you?

....

b) Will the fire burn all night long?

....

c) Will Paul wear his new suit?

....

3. Fais une liste de bonnes résolutions pour l'année prochaine.

Dis que :

a) tu apprendras tes leçons.

....

b) tu ne regarderas pas la télévision tous les jours.

....

c) tu diras toujours la vérité.

....

4. Écris la forme contractée de *will*.

a) We will not work together again.

....

b) She will be scared.

....

c) I will help you tomorrow.

....

d) Bobby will not guess!

....

EXERCICE 1

a) What will he do if Susan lies? (leave the house)
If Susan lies, he will leave (he'll leave) the house.

b) How will you feel if she comes with me? (be surprised)
If she comes with you, I will (I'll be) be surprised.

c) What will they do if we are late? (wait for us)
If we are late, they will wait (they'll wait) for us.

EXERCICE 2

a) If Lilly **doesn't hurry** up, we **will miss (we'll miss)** the train.

b) We **will see (we'll see)** the rocket if the weather **is** fine.

c) **Will** they **find** the house, if Nancy **forgets** to phone them?

EXERCICE 3

a) What will you do if they don't deliver the pizza?
If they don't deliver the pizza, I / we will cook spaghetti.

b) If she gets the job, when will she start?
If she gets the job, she will start on Monday.

24

IF + WILL

- ***If* sert à exprimer la condition.**

Il se traduit par « si ».
I will come if you want.
Je viendrai si tu veux.

- ***If* relie deux propositions.**

La proposition introduite par *if* est au présent simple. La proposition principale est au futur simple.
If it rains, we will not go out.
S'il pleut, nous ne sortirons pas.

- **Attention !**

Comme en français, la proposition introduite par *if* n'est jamais au futur simple : elle est au présent.

1. Réponds aux questions à l'aide des mots entre parenthèses.

Ex. : What will Neil do if he misses the train?
(take the next train) ***If Neil misses the train, he will take (he'll take) the next train.***

a) What will he do if Susan lies? (leave the house)

....

b) How will you feel if she comes with me? (be surprised)

....

c) What will they do if we are late? (wait for us)

....

2. Complète les phrases à l'aide des verbes entre parenthèses, conjugués au présent simple ou au futur simple.

a) If Lilly ....

(not hurry) up, we ....

(miss) the train.

b) We .... (see)

the rocket if the weather

.... (be) fine.

c) .... they

.... (find) the

house, if Nancy ....

(forget) to phone them?

3. Réponds aux questions en composant des phrases à l'aide des mots entre parenthèses.

Ex. : Where will Mark go if he gets money?
(to Italy) ***If Mark gets money, he will go to Italy.***

a) What will you do if they don't deliver the pizza?
(cook spaghetti) ....

....

b) If she gets the job, when will she start?
(on Monday) ....

....

EXERCICE 1

love	need	leave
understand	**hate**	want
like	suppose	**prefer**
live	believe	know

EXERCICE 2

a) Would you to prefer an ice cream?
Would you prefer an ice cream?

b) I will hate to be sick.
I would hate to be sick.

c) William wouldn't like lose.
William wouldn't like to lose.

d) Would like the Smith to meet us on the beach?
Would the Smiths like to meet us on the beach?

e) I will love to go away!
I would love to go away!

EXERCICE 3

a) live in the USA.
I would like / love / hate to live in the USA.

b) lose your watch.
I would like / love / hate to lose my watch.

c) have a horse.
I would like / love / hate to have a horse.

d) speak English fluently.
I would like / love / hate to speak English fluently.

EXERCICE 4

a) **Would you begin now?**
No, I wouldn't begin now.

b) **Would you like to brush your teeth immediately?**
Yes, I'd like to brush my teeth immediately.

c) **Would Steve hate to write novels?**
Yes, Steve would hate to write novels.

FORMES CONTRACTÉES

La contraction de *would* est *'d*.

I would like	*I'd like*
she would like	*she'd like*
they would like	*they'd like*

Dans les phrases négatives, la forme contractée est *wouldn't* à toutes les personnes.

He would not = He wouldn't

CE QUE L'ON AIMERAIT FAIRE OU PAS

I would like to leave.
J'aimerais partir.

I would love to go out.
J'aimerais vraiment beaucoup sortir.

I would hate to lose.
Je détesterais (cela me déplairait beaucoup de) perdre.

25 CONDITIONNEL – *WOULD*

● **Emploi.**

– Il sert à exprimer **une condition**.
I would be very happy.

– Il sert à exprimer **ce que l'on aimerait faire ou non**. Il est alors suivi d'un verbe à l'infinitif avec *to*.
I'd like to be a singer.
J'aimerais être chanteur.

● **Construction.**

Sujet + *would* + verbe à l'infinitif sans *to*
She would leave.

● **Questions.**

Would + sujet + verbe
Would you listen to him?

● **Phrases négatives.**

Sujet + *would* + *not* + verbe
I would not (wouldn't) say that.

1. Souligne les verbes qui permettent d'exprimer ce que l'on aime faire ou non.

love	need	leave
understand	hate	want
like	suppose	prefer
live	believe	know

2. Chaque phrase au conditionnel comporte une erreur. Souligne-la et corrige-la.

a) Would you to prefer an ice-cream?

....

b) I will hate to be sick.

....

c) William wouldn't like lose.

....

d) Would like the Smith to meet us on the beach?

....

....

e) I will love to go away!

....

3. Dis à ton correspondant, Richard, ce que tu aimerais faire ou non. Fais des phrases à l'aide de *like*, *love*, *hate*.

a) live in the USA.

....

b) lose your watch.

....

c) have a horse.

....

d) speak English fluently.

....

4. Trouve les questions qui correspondent aux réponses ci-dessous.

a) ....?
No, I wouldn't begin now.

b) ....?
Yes, I'd like to brush my teeth immediately.

c) ....?
Yes, Steve would hate to write novels.

EXERCICE 1

a) Write your surname!
Écris ton nom de famille

b) Write your first name!
Écris ton prénom

c) Draw a triangle!

d) Write the name of the capital city of Australia!
Canberra

e) Write your English teacher's name!
Écris le nom de ton professeur d'anglais

f) Cross out answer *d)* !
~~**Canberra**~~

g) Write the date!
January 8th *(par exemple)*

EXERCICE 2

a) **Be polite!**

b) **Don't eat all the chocolate bars!**

c) **Don't play with the new computer!**

d) **Brush your teeth!**

e) **Don't tease the dog!**

f) **Do your homework!**

g) **Don't be rude!**

26 IMPÉRATIF

- **Pour la 2e pers. du sing. et du pluriel**

– à la forme affirmative : base verbale

Stand up!
Lève-toi !

– à la forme négative : *don't* + base verbale

Don't move!
Ne bouge pas !

- **Pour la 1re pers. du pluriel**

– à la forme affirmative : *let* + complément + base verbale

Let's go to the restaurant!
Allons au restaurant !

Remarque
Let's est la forme contractée de *let us.*

– à la forme négative : *let* + complément + *not* + base verbale

Let's not stay here!
Ne restons pas ici !

1. Exécute les ordres suivants :

a) Write your surname!

....

b) Write your first name!

....

c) Draw a triangle!

....

d) Write the name of the capital city of Australia!

....

e) Write your English teacher's name!

....

f) Cross out answer *d)* !

....

g) Write the date!

....

> Un conseil :
> montre toujours ce que tu sais faire.
> Ainsi, tes résultats progresseront !

2. Donne des ordres à un enfant en utilisant le vocabulaire proposé ci-dessous :

put your feet on the table / be polite / eat all the chocolate bars / stand on the chair / play with the new computer / brush your teeth / tease the dog / do your homework / be rude.

Ex. : ***Don't put your feet on the table!***

a) ....!

b) ....!

c) ....!

d) ....!

e) ....!

f) ....!

g) ....!

EXERCICE 1

a) **Liza doesn't like skiing.**

b) **Liza loves ice-skating.**

c) **Liza likes dancing.**

EXERCICE 2

a) **Do you like playing football?**

b) **Do you like fishing?**

c) **Do you like watching TV?**

EXERCICE 3

a) **I love / I like / I prefer / I hate running.**

b) **I love / I like / I prefer / I hate roller skating.**

c) **I love / I like / I prefer / I hate swimming.**

27

GÉRONDIF

● Emploi.

On l'utilise pour **exprimer des goûts** (ce que l'on aime, préfère, déteste...) après des verbes tels que *to like, to prefer, to hate...*
I like cycling, but I hate walking.

● Construction.

Base verbale + *-ing*
to read (lire) = *reading* (lire, la lecture)
to ski (skier) = *skiing* (skier, le ski)

● Fonction.

– Il peut être sujet.
Horse riding is fun.

– Il peut être complément.
I love reading.

– Il peut donc se traduire par un nom ou par un verbe.

1. Dis ce que Liza adore (), aime (), n'aime pas () ou déteste () faire durant ses vacances.

Ex. : ***Liza hates playing tennis.***

a) ....
....

b) ....
....

c) ....
....

2. Ton correspondant arrive bientôt. Afin de préparer vos vacances, pose-lui des questions sur ses goûts en utilisant les verbes suivants : *to play football / to fish / to watch TV.*

Ex. : ***Do you like walking?***

a) ....
b) ....
c) ....

3. Écris maintenant trois phrases concernant tes propres goûts en utilisant les verbes suivants : *to run / to roller skate / to swim.*

a) ....
b) ....
c) ....

QUELQUES VERBES À PARTICULES

to look for : chercher
to look after : s'occuper de (un malade, un enfant)
to take off : décoller (pour un avion) ; enlever (un vêtement, des chaussures)
to take back : reprendre (un objet)
to take away : emporter
to turn on : allumer (le chauffage, le gaz, la lumière)
to turn off : éteindre (le chauffage, le gaz, la lumière)
to put on : mettre (un vêtement, des chaussures)

b) **to look for**

c) **to put on**

EXERCICE 1

a) **to turn off**

EXERCICE 2

to talk • • away
to take • • on
to pay • • about
to turn • • for

EXERCICE 3

a) Dis que l'avion décolle à 10 heures.
The plane takes off at 10 o'clock.

b) Dis que tu ne peux pas toujours t'occuper de ton frère.
I can't always look after my brother.

c) Dis que tu voudrais reprendre ton livre.
I'd like to take my book back.

d) Dis que tu ne veux pas mettre ton manteau.
I don't want to put my coat on *ou* **I don't want to put on my coat.**

28 VERBES À PARTICULES

● **Certains verbes sont suivis d'une particule.**

*To pay **for**, to laugh **at**, to look **at**, to speak **about**.*

Look at me!
Regarde-moi !

I was speaking about them.
Je parlais d'eux.

● **La particule peut modifier le sens du verbe.**

To look : regarder
*To look **after*** : s'occuper de
*To look **for*** : chercher

● **Forme interrogative.**

Dans une question,
la particule se place en fin de phrase.
*What are you looking **for**?*
*Who are they talking **about**?*

1. Écris le verbe correspondant à chacun de ces dessins.

Reporte-toi au vocabulaire de la p. 62.

a) ....

b) ....

c) ....

2. Relie chaque verbe avec sa particule.

to talk ▪	▪ away
to take ▪	▪ on
to pay ▪	▪ about
to turn ▪	▪ for

3. Comment dirais-tu que :

a) l'avion décolle à 10 heures.

....

b) tu ne peux pas toujours t'occuper de ton frère.

....

....

c) tu voudrais reprendre ton livre.

....

....

d) tu ne veux pas mettre ton manteau.

....

....

EXERCICE 1

a) **Can you speak French? No, I can't.**

b) **Can you jump over a fence? No, I can't.**

c) **Can you drive? No, I can't.**

d) **Can you play chess? Yes, I can.**

e) **Can you cook? Yes, I can.**

EXERCICE 2

a) **Stan can't speak French.**

b) **Stan can't jump over a fence.**

c) **Stan can't drive.**

d) **Stan can play chess.**

e) **Stan can cook.**

EXERCICE 3

a) **Can I go to the cinema?**

b) **Can I stay in bed?**

c) **Can I call Sarah?**

d) **Can I buy a new CD?**

e) **Can I borrow your book?**

29

CAN / CAN'T

Pour exprimer :

- **la possibilité, la capacité à faire quelque chose :**

(« pouvoir », « être capable de », « savoir »).
Can you ski ? No, I can't.
Helen can ride a horse but she can't drive a car.

- **la permission :**

Can I go now?
Yes, you can. / No, you can't.

Remarque
Can't est la contraction de *cannot* et correspond à la forme négative.

- ***Can* est un auxiliaire .**

Il n'est jamais suivi de *to* ou *-ing*.

1. Voici des informations concernant ce que Stan sait faire ou non. Pose-lui des questions et écris ses réponses, comme dans l'exemple.

Use a word processor	yes
Speak French	no
Jump over a fence	no
Drive	no
Play chess	yes
Cook	yes

Ex. : ***Can you use a word processor? Yes, I can.***

a) ....

b) ....

c) ....

d) ....

e) ....

2. En reprenant les informations ci-dessus, raconte maintenant à un camarade ce que Stan sait faire ou non.

Ex. : ***Stan can use a word processor.***

a) ....

b) ....

c) ....

d) ....

e) ....

3. Demande la permission de faire les choses suivantes : *invite friends / go to the cinema / stay in bed / call Sarah / buy a new CD / borrow your book*

Ex. : ***Can I invite friends?***

a) ....

b) ....

c) ....

d) ....

e) ....

EXERCICE 1

a) You **mustn't** loose your key again!

b) You **must** sweep the floor because it's dirty!

c) You **mustn't** smoke!

d) You **mustn't** invite all your friends because they're noisy!

e) You **mustn't** watch TV all day, because you **must** clean the house!

EXERCICE 2

a) I **had to cook** dinner!

b) I **had to wash** the dishes!

c) I **had to help** my sister with her homework!

d) I **had to make** all the beds!

e) I **had to read** stories to my baby brother!

EXERCICE 3

a) The children must read this book!
The children will have to read this book!

b) She must answer the phone!
She will have to answer the phone!

c) You must start this exercise !
You will have to start this exercise!

d) He must do the shopping!
He will have to do the shopping!

e) They must stay at home!
They will have to stay at home!

30 MUST / MUSTN'T / HAVE TO

- ***Must*** **: pour exprimer un ordre.**

You must shut the door immediately!
Tu dois fermer la porte immédiatement !

- ***Mustn't*** **: pour exprimer une interdiction.**

She mustn't lock the dog!
Elle ne doit pas enfermer le chien !

- ***Have to*** **: pour exprimer une obligation.**

– Au présent. Il a un sens moins fort que ***must***.
– Au passé et au futur, on doit utiliser *have to* car ***must*** n'existe pas.
I had to tidy my bedroom.
J'ai dû ranger ma chambre.
You'll have to do the washing up.
Tu devras faire la vaisselle.

1. Complète les consignes que t'ont données tes parents avant de partir travailler. Utilise *must* ou *mustn't*.

a) You .... lose your key again!

b) You .... sweep the floor because it's dirty!

c) You .... smoke!

d) You .... invite all your friends because they're noisy!

e) You .... watch TV all

day, because you .... clean the house!

2. Au téléphone, dis à une amie pourquoi tu n'as pas pu aller chez elle hier. Utilise les verbes suivants : *to wash / to help / to read / to make / to cook / to clean*.

*Ex. : I **had to clean** the windows!*

a) I .... dinner!

b) I .... the dishes!

c) I .... my sister with her homework!

d) I .... all the beds!

e) I .... stories to my baby brother!

3. Mets les phrases suivantes au futur.

a) The children must read this book!

....

b) She must answer the phone!

....

c) You must start this exercise!

....

d) He must do the shopping!

....

e) They must stay at home!

....

EXERCICE 1

a) **The day before yesterday, he didn't have to sign autographs in Seattle.**

b) **Yesterday, he didn't have to fly to Dallas.**

c) **Tomorrow, he will not have to be in London.**

d) **The day after tomorrow, he will not have to go back home.**

EXERCICE 2

a) **She doesn't need to go to work. / She needn't go to work.**

b) **She doesn't need to take the bus. / She needn't take the bus.**

c) **She doesn't need to get up early. / She needn't get up early.**

d) **She doesn't need to cook. / She needn't cook.**

Attention !

En anglais, les noms des jours et des mois s'écrivent avec une majuscule.
Ex. : Monday 1st of March.

Tu n'es pas obligé(e) de trouver ce chapitre difficile...
En te concentrant un peu, tu découvriras qu'il est facile!

31 DON'T HAVE TO / NEEDN'T

● ***Don't have to* : pour exprimer l'absence d'obligation.**

– Au présent.

You don't have to work now.
Tu n'es pas obligé de travailler maintenant.

– Au passé.

She didn't have to come.
Elle n'était pas obligée de venir.

– Au futur.

They won't have to hurry.
Ils ne seront pas obligés de se dépêcher.

● ***Needn't* : pour exprimer l'absence de nécessité.**

Deux constructions possibles :

You needn't buy this book. / You don't need to buy this book.
Tu n'as pas besoin d'acheter ce livre.

1. La tournée de Tony Mangano, le chanteur, a été annulée. Explique ce qu'il n'était pas, n'est pas ou ne sera pas obligé de faire. Nous sommes aujourd'hui le 23 mai.

Ex. : *Today,* ***he doesn't have to meet a new guitarist.***

a) The day before yesterday, ...

....

b) Yesterday, ...

....

c) Tomorrow, ...

....

d) The day after tomorrow, ...

....

2. Dis ce que Wanda, la femme de Tony, n'a pas besoin de faire.

Ex. : wash the dishes
She doesn't need to wash the dishes.

a) go to work

....

....

b) take the bus

....

....

c) get up early

....

....

d) cook

....

....

EXERCICE 1

a) **He must be happy.**

b) **He must be angry.**

c) **He must be surprised.**

d) **He must be sad.**

EXERCICE 2

Dis :

a) que Brian doit être malade.
Brian must be ill.

b) qu'il se peut que tes amis viennent ce soir.
My friends may come tonight / this evening.

c) qu'il se peut qu'il pleuve demain.
It may rain tomorrow.

d) que John doit être à Londres.
John must be in London.

e) qu'il doit faire chaud en Espagne.
It must be hot in Spain.

32 DEGRÉS DE CERTITUDE

- **Pour exprimer une certitude :**

– *must.*
She must be sad.
Elle doit être triste.

– *I'm sure / I'm certain.*
I'm sure it will rain tomorrow.
Je suis sûr qu'il pleuvra demain.

- **Pour exprimer une possibilité, une éventualité :**

– *may.*
I may go to Hawaii.
Il se peut que j'aille à Hawaii.

- **Attention !**

N'utilise jamais *to* derrière *may* et *must* ; ne mets jamais le verbe à la forme en *-ing*.

1. À l'aide des éléments ci-dessous, trouve une légende pour chaque dessin.
Happy / surprised / sad / angry.

Ex. : ***He must be sorry.***

a) ....

....

b) ....

....

c) ....

....

d) ....

....

2. Comment dirais-tu :

a) que Brian doit être malade.

....

....

b) qu'il se peut que tes amis viennent ce soir.

....

....

c) qu'il se peut qu'il pleuve demain.

....

....

d) que John doit être à Londres.

....

e) qu'il doit faire chaud en Espagne.

....

EXERCICE 1

a) **Why** are you crying?

b) **Where**'s your family?

c) **Who**'s that? Your sister?

d) **What** would you like to drink? An orange juice?

e) **When** did you see Helen? Last Friday?

f) **How** are you? Fine?

EXERCICE 2

a) I come from ? ? ? ? ? ? ? ? ? ? ? ? ?
Where do you come from?

b) I arrived last ? ? ? ? ? ? ? ? ? ? ? ? ?
When did you arrive?

c) I always travel with ? ? ? ? ? ? ? ?
Who do you always travel with?

d) I go to Los Angeles every ? ? ? ?
When do you go to Los Angeles?

e) I'm learning ? ? ? ? ? ? ? ? ? ? ? ? ?
What are you learning?

f) I'm laughing because ? ? ? ? ? ? ?
Why are you laughing?

LES PRONOMS INTERROGATIFS

what	que, qu', quoi
where	où
when	quand
how	comment
who	qui
why	pourquoi
whose	à qui, de qui

33 PHRASE INTERROGATIVE

Les phrases interrogatives se construisent à l'aide des pronoms interrogatifs.

- **Le pronom interrogatif se place au début d'une phrase à la forme interrogative.**

Pron. interrog. + aux.
+ sujet + verbe
Why is he leaving ?
Pourquoi part-il ?

- **Si le verbe est accompagné d'une préposition, celle-ci se place à la fin de la question.**

***Who** will you come **with**?*
***Where** do you come **from**?*

1. Complète les phrases suivantes avec le pronom interrogatif qui convient.

a) .... are you crying?
(why / where / how)

b) ....'s your family?
(when / where / what)

c) ....'s that? Your sister?
(what / who / where)

d) .... would you like to drink? An orange juice?
(what / where / when)

e) .... did you see Helen? Last Friday?
(when / who / how)

f) .... are you? Fine?
(where / how / why)

2. Lors d'une soirée, un Anglais t'adresse la parole. Tu n'entends pas tout ce qu'il te dit car il y a trop de bruit. Pose-lui des questions.

Ex. : I live in ? ? ? ? ? ? ? ? ? ? ? ?
Where do you live?

a) I come from ? ? ? ? ? ? ? ? ? ? ? ? ?

.... ?

b) I arrived last ? ? ? ? ? ? ? ? ? ? ? ? ?

.... ?

c) I always travel with ? ? ? ? ? ? ? ? ?

.... ?

d) I go to Los Angeles every ? ? ? ? ?

.... ?

e) I'm learning ? ? ? ? ? ? ? ? ? ? ? ? ?

.... ?

f) I'm laughing because ? ? ? ? ? ? ? ?

.... ?

EXERCICE 1

a) **What an** interesting story!

b) **How** stupid you are! I can't believe it!

c) **What a** poor guy!

EXERCICE 2

a) That cupboard is very big.
What a big cupboard!
How big that cupboard is!

b) This dish is delicious.
What a delicious dish!
How delicious this dish is!

c) His blazer is very small.
What a small blazer!
How small his blazer is!

d) She's a crazy girl.
What a crazy girl!
How crazy that / this girl is!

EXERCICE 3

a) **What a terrible** smell!

b) **What an** enormous breakfast **you are having**!

c) What **a pity**!

d) **How** lazy **they are**!

e) **How boring** this film was!

34 PHRASE EXCLAMATIVE

Pour exprimer l'étonnement ou l'exclamation :

- ***how* + adjectif ou adverbe.**

How amazing that story is!
Comme cette histoire est incroyable !

Remarque
Il n'y a pas d'inversion du sujet et du verbe car il ne s'agit pas d'une question.
How far it is! / How far is it?
Comme c'est loin ! / À quelle distance est-ce ?

- ***what a* + nom ou groupe nominal.**

What a big house! What an awful story!
Quelle grande maison ! Quelle horrible histoire !

- **Le sujet et le verbe peuvent être sous-entendus.**

How funny!
What a stupid idea!

1. Complète les phrases à l'aide de *how, what a* ou *what an.*

a) .... interesting story!

b) .... stupid you are! I can't believe it!

c) .... poor guy!

2. Transforme les phrases suivantes comme dans l'exemple.

Ex. : That hotel is very comfortable.
What a comfortable hotel!
How comfortable that hotel is!

a) That cupboard is very big.

....!

....!

b) This dish is delicious.

....!

....!

c) His blazer is very small.

....!

....!

d) She's a crazy girl.

....!

....!

3. Fais cinq phrases à l'aide des mots proposés ci-dessous. Chaque case ne peut être utilisée qu'une fois. Certains mots ont été déjà placés dans les phrases pour t'aider !

???????	what	they	???????
you	boring	an	lazy
are	terrible	?????????	what
smell	breakfast	a	having
???????	how	pity	what
are	was	film	????????
that	????????	enormous	how

a) .... smell !

b) .... enormous breakfast ....!

c) What ....!

d) .... lazy ....!

e) .... this film was !

EXERCICE 1

a) How about **going** to the swimming-pool?

b) Shall we **leave** our bags here?

c) Let's **sing** now!

d) We could **climb** up that mountain tomorrow!

e) What about **learning** Japanese next term?

EXERCICE 2

a) **What about / how about** playing cards?

b) We **could** listen to music!

c) **Let's / we could** do cross-words!

d) **Shall** we watch TV?

e) **What about / how about** reading comics?

EXERCICE 3

a) let / go / 's / roller skating / !
Let's go roller skating!

b) we / ? / out / shall / go
Shall we go out?

c) the / riding / ? / what / on / beach / about
What about riding on the beach?

d) your / about / this / how / repairing / bike / ? / afternoon
How about repairing your bike this afternoon?

e) could / we / ! / swimming / go / Thursday / next
We could go swimming next Thursday!

35 SUGGESTION

Pour suggérer une activité :

- ***What about* + *-ing.***

What about phoning Tom?
Et si on appelait Tom ?

- ***How about* + *-ing.***

How about taking the bus?
Et si on prenait l'autobus ?

- ***Shall we* + verbe à l'infinitif sans *to*.**

Shall we dance?
On danse ?

- ***Could.***

We could organize a picnic!
On pourrait organiser un pique-nique !

- ***Let's.***

Let's go!
Allons-y !
Il s'agit de l'impératif (voir chapitre 26).

1. Réécris les phrases en corrigeant les erreurs.

a) How about go to the swimming-pool?

....

b) Shall we leaving our bags here?

....

c) Let's singing now!

....

d) We could climbing up that mountain tomorrow!

....

e) What about learn Japanese next term?

....

2. Kathy s'est cassé la jambe et ne peut pas sortir. Propose-lui des activités.

a) .... playing cards?

b) We .... listen to music!

c) .... do crosswords!

d) .... we watch TV?

e) .... reading comics?

3. Fais des phrases en remettant les mots dans l'ordre.

a) let / go / 's / roller skating / !

....

b) we / ? / out / shall / go

....

c) the / riding / ? / what / on / beach / about

....

....

d) your / about / this / how / repairing / bike / ? / afternoon

....

....

e) could / we / ! / swimming / go / Thursday / next

....

....

EXERCICE 1

a) « I can't come. »
Jimmy said he couldn't come.
(➜ *Au discours indirect,* can *devient* could.)

b) « I'll come tomorrow. »
Jimmy said he would come tomorrow.
(➜ *Au discours indirect, le futur devient un conditionnel présent.)*

c) « We can go to the cinema.»
Jimmy said we / you could go to the cinema.

d) « I'll buy you an ice-cream. »
Jimmy said he would buy you / me an ice cream.

e) « I can meet Al and Val. »
Jimmy said he could meet Al and Val.

EXERCICE 2

a) He asked where his bag was.
« Where is my bag? »

b) The teacher asked what time it was.
« What time is it? »

c) He asked what my name was.
« What is your name? »

d) James asked if I could help him.
« Can you help me? »

e) Alan asked if I was in love with Marge.
« Are you in love with Marge? »

EXERCICE 3

a) Meg / she / sorry / said / was / .
Meg said she was sorry.

b) Ken / could / if / I / write / asked / to / him / .
Ken asked if I could write to him.

c) Jeff / likes / playing / says / he/ darts / .
Jeff says he likes playing darts.

d) Ricardo / did / ask / if / would / Sam / here / be / ?
Did Ricardo ask if Sam would be here?

36 DISCOURS INDIRECT

- **Pour rapporter des propos :**

– au présent : *« I'm happy. »*
John says he is happy.
– au passé : attention au changement de temps.
« I'm sorry. »
(présent)
John said he was sorry.
(prétérit)

« I'll see you soon. »
(futur)
John said he would see you soon.
(conditionnel présent)

« I can swim. »
(can)
John said he could swim.
(could)

- **Pour rapporter des questions :**

« Is James in bed? » He asked if John was in bed.
On utilise une tournure affirmative.

1. Jimmy a appelé et laissé un message pour ta sœur. Retransmets le message.

Ex. : « I'll go to the swimming-pool this evening. »
He said he would go to the swimming-pool this evening.

a) « I can't come. »

....

b) « I'll come and see you tomorrow. »

....

c) « We can go to the cinema. »

....

d) « I'll buy you an ice cream. »

....

e) « I can meet Al and Val. »

....

2. Retrouve les questions qui ont été posées.

a) He asked where his bag was.

« ....? »

b) The teacher asked what time it was.

« ....? »

c) He asked what my name was.

« ....? »

d) James asked if I could help him.

« ....? »

e) Alan asked if I was in love with Marge.

« ....? »

3. Remets les mots dans l'ordre afin de faire une phrase correcte.

a) Meg / she / sorry / said / was / .

....

b) Ken / could / if / I / write / asked / to / him / .

....

c) Jeff / likes / playing / says / he / darts / .

....

d) Ricardo / did / ask / if / would / Sam / here / be / ?

....

EXERCICE 1

a) Bruce's from Toronto ; **he**'s Canadian.

b) Sandra's a baby ; **she**'s two years old!

c) Jerry and I work in that school ; **we**'re teachers.

d) Olga and Ryan are students ; **they** go to university.

e) My name's Joe ; **I**'m from New Zealand.

f) Do **you** like apple pie? Yes, I do.

EXERCICE 2

a) I'm going to the swimming pool with Eric. Come with **us**!

b) Mr Hall is our new maths teacher. We like **him** very much.

c) They love football. I often play with **them**.

d) Stan loves Patty and he wants to marry **her**.

e) I'm talking. Please listen to **me**.

f) Mrs Dale is shouting at Jenny. She's angry with **her**!

EXERCICE 3

a) Sue went to Paris with **us**.

b) **He** doesn't like coke.

c) **We** were very happy here.

d) Please help **him**.

e) Did Sally travel with **you**?

f) Does **she** like swimming?

LES PRONOMS PERSONNELS SUJETS

I	je
you	tu
he	il
she	elle
it	il, elle (neutre)
we	nous
you	vous
they	ils, elles

LES PRONOMS PERSONNELS COMPLÉMENTS DIRECTS ET INDIRECTS

me	me, moi
you	te, toi
him	le, lui
her	la, lui, elle
it	le, la, lui (neutre)
us	nous
you	vous
them	les, leur, eux

37 PRONOMS PERSONNELS SUJETS / COMPLÉMENTS

- **Pronoms personnels sujets.**

– À la 3e personne du singulier :
he pour le **masculin**,
she pour le **féminin**,
it pour le **neutre** (objets, animaux non domestiques).

– À la 2e personne :
you au singulier et au pluriel. Il n'y a donc pas de distinction entre « tu » et « vous ».

- **Pronoms personnels compléments.**

– Ils se placent après le verbe.
– À la 3e personne du singulier, on emploie
him pour le **masculin**,
her pour le **féminin** et
it pour le **neutre**.

1. Complète les phrases à l'aide du pronom personnel sujet qui convient.

a) Bruce's from Toronto ; ....'s Canadian.

b) Sandra's a baby ; ....'s two years old !

c) Jerry and I work in that school ; ....'re teachers.

d) Olga and Ryan are students ; .... go to university.

e) My name's Joe ; ....'m from New Zealand.

f) Do .... like apple pie ? Yes, I do.

2. Complète les phrases à l'aide du pronom personnel complément qui convient.

a) I'm going to the swimming pool with Eric. Come with ....!

b) Mr Hall is our new maths teacher. We like .... very much.

c) They love football. I often play with ....

d) Stan loves Patty and he wants to marry ....

e) I'm talking. Please listen to ....

f) Mrs Dale is shouting at Jenny. She's angry with .... !

3. Parmi les pronoms personnels indiqués entre parenthèses, choisis celui qui convient pour compléter les phrases.

a) Sue went to Paris with .... (I /us)

b) .... doesn't like coke. (we / he)

c) .... were very happy here. (we / us)

d) Please help .... (he / him)

e) Did Sally travel with ....? (you /his)

f) Does .... like swimming? (she /her)

EXERCICE 1

a) I carried my luggage **myself**. Nobody helped me.

b) Now go, wash and brush your teeth!

c) Can we help them? No, they want to do it **themselves**.

d) Larry never shaves on Sundays.

e) Did you look at **yourself / yourselves** in the mirror this morning?

f) He cut **himself** this morning.

LES PRONOMS RÉFLÉCHIS

myself	moi-même, me
yourself	toi-même, te
himself	lui-même, se
herself	elle-même, se
itself	lui-même, se (neutre)
ourselves	nous-mêmes, nous
yourselves	vous-même, vous
themselves	eux-mêmes, se

EXERCICE 2

a) James always does my home-work.
But you **can do it yourself**!

b) Ben's mother always tidies his bedroom.
But he **can tidy it himself**!

c) Their parents will organize the birthday party.
But they **can organize it themselves**!

d) Oscar always carries Meg's schoolbag.
But she **can carry it herself**!

e) I'll do the shopping for you.
But we **can do it ourselves**!

f) I want to talk to your father.
But I **can talk to him myself**!

EXERCICE 3

se rencontrer •	• to go to bed
se battre •	• to wake up
se lever •	• to meet
se coucher •	• to fight
se réveiller •	• to get up

(se rencontrer → to meet; se battre → to fight; se lever → to get up; se coucher → to go to bed; se réveiller → to wake up)

38 PRONOMS RÉFLÉCHIS

● **Emploi.**

– On peut les utiliser pour traduire certains **verbes pronominaux** en français.
I looked at myself in the mirror.
Je me suis regardé(e) dans le miroir.

– On peut les utiliser pour insister sur ce qu'on a fait **soi-même**.
I made that cake myself.
J'ai fait ce gâteau moi-même.

● **Attention !**

Les verbes pronominaux en français ne nécessitent pas toujours l'utilisation d'un pronom réfléchi en anglais. C'est par exemple le cas des verbes suivants : « se lever », « se raser », « se laver ». En anglais, ils ne sont pas suivis d'un pronom réfléchi.

1. Complète les phrases en utilisant un pronom réfléchi, si nécessaire.

a) I carried my luggage .... Nobody helped me.

b) Now go, wash .... and brush .... your teeth!

c) Can we help them? No, they want to do it ....

d) Larry never shaves .... on Sundays.

e) Did you look at .... in the mirror this morning?

f) He cut .... this morning.

2. Réagis à ce que te dit ton ami, comme dans l'exemple.

Ex. : Sam will post these letters for Sarah.
But she ***can post them herself!***

a) James always does my homework.

But you ....!

b) Ben's mother always tidies his bedroom.

But he ....!

c) Their parents will organize the birthday party.

But they ....!

d) Oscar always carries Meg's schoolbag.

But she ....!

e) I'll do the shopping for you.

But we ....!

f) I want to talk to your father.

But I ....!

3. Relie les verbes en français à leur équivalent anglais.

Attention : ces verbes sont pronominaux en français mais ne sont pas suivis d'un pronom réfléchi en anglais.

se rencontrer ▪	▪ to go to bed
se battre ▪	▪ to wake up
se lever ▪	▪ to meet
se coucher ▪	▪ to fight
se réveiller ▪	▪ to get up

EXERCICE 2

a) (small) **Ben's house is smaller than Steve's.**

b) (cheap) **Ben's house is cheaper than Steve's.**

c) (comfortable) **Steve's house is more comfortable than Ben's.**

d) (noisy) **Ben's house is noisier than Steve's.**

e) (nice) **Steve's house is nicer than Ben's.**

EXERCICE 1

Adjectifs courts	Comparatifs	Adjectifs longs	Comparatifs
deep	**deeper**	**dangerous**	**more dangerous**
fast	**faster**	**useful**	**more useful**
heavy	**heavier**	**comfortable**	**more comfortable**
nice	**nicer**	**interesting**	**more interesting**

39 COMPARATIF DE SUPÉRIORITÉ

● Adjectifs courts :

1 syllabe ou 2 syllabes (terminés par *-y, -ow, -e*).
adjectif + *-er* + *than*
I'm taller than you.
Je suis plus grand que toi.

Attention à l'orthographe !

nice	*nic**er***
pretty	*pret**tier***
big	*big**ger***

● Adjectifs longs :

2 syllabes ou plus.
more + adjectif + *than*
He's more intelligent than them.
Il est plus intelligent qu'eux.

● Comparatifs irréguliers :

good	*better*
bad	*worse*

1. Classe les adjectifs suivants et leur comparatif de supériorité dans la bonne colonne : *deep / dangerous / fast / heavy / useful / nice / comfortable / interesting.*

Adjectifs courts	Comparatifs
....	....
....	....
....	....
....	....

Adjectifs longs	Comparatifs
....	....
....	....
....	....
....	....

2. Compare les maisons de Ben et de Steve à l'aide des adjectifs proposés. Utilise un comparatif de supériorité.

Tu peux réviser le chapitre 47 avant de faire cet exercice.

Ex. : (old) ***Ben's house is older than Steve's.***

a) (smal) ....
....

b) (cheap) ....
....

c) (comfortable) ....
....

d) (noisy) ....
....

e) (nice) ....
....

EXERCICE 1

a) (strong) **Alex isn't as strong as Bob.**

b) (fat) **Alex isn't as fat as Bob.**

c) (nice) **Alex isn't as nice as Bob.**

EXERCICE 2

a) as / famous / the Spice Girls / Prince Charles / is / as / the / ?
Is Prince Charles as famous as the Spice Girls?

b) isn't / England / big / as / as / Argentina / .
England isn't as big as Argentina.

c) yours / daddy / my / as / ! / is / strong / as
My daddy is as strong as yours!

d) beautiful / isn't / as / Sarah / sisters / as / her / .
Sarah isn't as beautiful as her sisters.

e) those / biscuits / is / that / chocolates / box / as / of / ? / expensive / as
Is that box of chocolates as expensive as those biscuits?

Ton envie de travailler
est-elle aussi forte
que ton envie de réussir?

40 COMPARATIF D'ÉGALITÉ

La construction est la même pour les adjectifs courts ou longs.

- **À la forme affirmative (« aussi … que ») :**

as + adjectif + *as*
He's as clever as his sister.
Il est aussi intelligent que sa sœur.

- **À la forme négative (« pas aussi … que ») :**

not as + adjectif + *as*
Paris is not as expensive as Hong Kong.
Paris n'est pas aussi cher que Hong Kong.

1. Compare les personnages. Utilise uniquement des comparatifs d'égalité.

Ex. : (tall) ***Bob isn't as tall as Alex.***

a) (strong) ....

....

b) (fat) ....

....

c) (nice) ....

....

2. Remets les phrases suivantes dans le bon ordre.

a) as / famous / the Spice Girls / Prince Charles / is / as / the / ?

....

....

b) isn't / England / big / as / as / Argentina / .

....

....

c) yours / daddy / my / as / ! / is / strong / as

....

....

d) beautiful / isn't / as / Sarah / sisters / as / her / .

....

....

e) those / biscuits / is / that / chocolates / box / as / of / ? / expensive / as

....

....

EXERCICE 1

Adjectifs courts	Superlatifs
high	**the highest**
light	**the lightest**
rude	**the rudest**
hard	**the hardest**
Adjectifs longs	Superlatifs
delicious	**the most delicious**
patient	**the most patient**
expensive	**the most expensive**
dangerous	**the most dangerous**

Rappel
Tu dois toujours faire la différence entre les **adjectifs courts** et les **adjectifs longs**.

EXERCICE 2

a) Mexico City is **the biggest** city I know.
(➜ big *est un adjectif court.)*

b) I think geography is **the most interesting** subject in school.
(➜ interesting *est un adjectif long.)*

c) Carla is **the most beautiful** girl in my school.
(➜ beautiful *est un adjectif long.)*

d) Greg is **the strongest** in his football team.

EXERCICE 3

a) Tom is the goodest student at maths.
Tom is the **best** student at maths.
(➜ best *est le superlatif irrégulier de* good.*)*

b) Mr Brown is the most smart person I know.
Mr Brown is the **smartest** person I know.

c) The Sears Tower in Chicago isn't the most high skyscraper in the world!
The Sears Tower in Chicago isn't the **highest** skyscraper in the world!

d) Hungarian is one of the difficultest languages to learn.
Hungarian is one of the **most difficult** languages to learn.

41 SUPERLATIF DE SUPÉRIORITÉ

● **Adjectifs courts :**

1 syllabe ou 2 syllabes (terminés par *-y, -ow, -e*).
the + adjectif + *est*
Franck is the brightest in the group.
Franck est le plus brillant dans le groupe.

Attention à l'orthographe !

nice	*the nic**est***
tidy	*the tid**iest***
dirty	*the dirt**iest***
big	*the big**gest***

● **Adjectifs longs :**

2 syllabes ou plus.
the most + adjectif
He's the most competent.
Il est le plus compétent.

● **Superlatifs irréguliers :**

good	*the best*
bad	*the worst*

1. Classe les adjectifs suivants et leurs superlatifs dans la bonne colonne : *delicious / high / light / patient / expensive / rude / hard / dangerous.*

Adjectifs courts	Superlatifs
....	....
....	....
....	....
....	....

Adjectifs longs	Superlatifs
....	....
....	....
....	....
....	....

2. Mets les adjectifs entre parenthèses au superlatif.

a) Mexico City is (big) .... city I know.

b) I think geography is (interesting) .... subject in school.

c) Carla is (beautiful) .... girl in my school.

d) Greg is (strong) .... in his football team.

3. Chaque phrase comporte une erreur. Souligne-la et corrige-la.

a) Tom is the goodest student at maths.

....

b) Mr Brown is the most smart person I know.

....

c) The Sears Tower in Chicago isn't the most high skyscraper in the world!

....

d) Hungarian is one of the difficultest languages to learn.

....

EXERCICE 1

a) **This is a skirt and that's a dress.**
(➜ Regarde le dessin : la jupe est au premier plan et la robe est plus loin.)

b) **These are shoes and those are slippers.**
(➜ Même remarque.)

EXERCICE 2

a) These are my shirts.
This is my shirt.

b) Those are my books.
That's my book.

c) Do you like those pictures on the wall?
Do you like that picture on the wall?

d) How much are these please?
How much is this please?

e) Are these seats free?
Is this seat free?

EXERCICE 3

a) Can you see **those** pictures over there?

b) Who's **that** girl in the car on the road?

c) **Those** stars are very far.

d) **This** is Golden Gate.

e) **Those** are my best friends.

42 THIS / THAT / THESE / THOSE

● **Emploi.**

Les adjectifs et pronoms démonstratifs servent à désigner un objet ou une personne.

● **Si l'on est près *(here)* :**

– ***this*** **au singulier.**
I don't like this dress ; this isn't a very nice dress.

– ***these*** **au pluriel.**
I like these people; these are very nice people.

● **Si l'on est loin *(there, over there)* :**

– ***that*** **au singulier.**
I like that girl; that's a nice girl.

– ***those*** **au pluriel.**
I don't like those shoes ; those are ugly shoes.

1. Rédige la légende de chaque dessin, en utilisant *this, that, these* et *those*.

a) *b)*

a) .... and
....

b) .... and
....

2. Mets les phrases suivantes au singulier.

a) These are my shirts.
....

b) Those are my books.
....

c) Do you like those pictures on the wall?
....

d) How much are these please?
....

e) Are these seats free?
....

3. Complète les phrases avec l'adjectif ou le pronom démonstratif qui convient, parmi ceux proposés entre parenthèses.

a) Can you see .... pictures over there? (those / these / that)

b) Who's .... girl in the car on the road? (those / that / these)

c) .... stars are very far. (these / those / that)

d) .... is Golden Gate Bridge. (this / those / these)

e) .... are my best friends. (that / those / this)

EXERCICE 1

SINGULIER	PLURIEL
one tomato	**two tomatoes**
one box	**two boxes**
one leaf	two leaves
one baby	**two babies**
one shelf	**two shelves**
one wife	two wives
one mouse	two mice

EXERCICE 2

a) How many childs did you invite?
How many children did you invite?
(➜ children *est le pluriel irrégulier de* child.)

b) There is one churches in our town.
There is one church in our town.

c) Our cat always catches a lot of mouse.
Our cat always catches a lot of mice.
(➜ mice *est le pluriel irrégulier de* mouse.)

d) Please send a replies by e-mail.
Please send a reply by e-mail.

e) There are many leafs on the ground.
There are many leaves on the ground.
(➜ *Attention à la modification orthographique.)*

f) You need a knive if you want to cut that branch.
You need a knife if you want to cut that branch.

g) Where did you buy your furnitures?
Where did you buy your furniture?
(➜ furniture *est toujours au singulier. C'est un indénombrable.)*

EXERCICE 3

Dis que :

a) ton pyjama n'est pas sur ton lit.
My pyjamas aren't on my bed.

b) ton pantalon préféré est bleu.
My favourite trousers / pants are blue.

c) tes bagages sont lourds.
My luggage is heavy.

d) Les nouvelles ne sont pas très bonnes ce matin.
The news isn't very good this morning.

LES PLURIELS IRRÉGULIERS

one man	*two men*
one woman	*two women*
one foot	*two feet*
one mouse	*two mice*
one child	*two children*
one tooth	*two teeth*

– Mots en *f, fe, lf*

one leaf	*two leaves*
one knife	*two knives*
one shelf	*two shelves*

– Mots en *s, x, z, ch, sh, o, y*

one box	*two boxes*
one dress	*two dresses*
one sandwich	*two sandwiches*
one potato	*two potatoes*
one country	*two countries*

43 NOMS SINGULIERS / PLURIELS

Formation du pluriel.

On ajoute un ***s*** au singulier.
a dog / dogs

Attention, il y a des exceptions ! (voir liste p. 92)

Noms toujours au singulier :

luggage (les bagages), *furniture* (les meubles), *news* (les nouvelles)
The news is good.
Les nouvelles sont bonnes.

Noms toujours au pluriel :

people (les gens), *police* (la police), *scissors* (les ciseaux), *trousers* (GB) / *pants* (US) (le pantalon), *pyjamas* (le pyjama), *shorts* (le short).
My trousers are too old.
Mon pantalon est trop vieux.
The police are here.
La police est ici.

1. Complète le tableau ci-dessous.

SINGULIER	PLURIEL
one tomato	....
one box	....
....	two leaves
one baby	....
one shelf	....
....	two wives
....	two mice

2. Souligne les erreurs et réécris les phrases correctement.

a) How many childs did you invite?

....

b) There is one churches in our town.

....

c) Our cat always catches a lot of mouse.

....

d) Please send a replies by e-mail.

....

e) There are many leafs on the ground.

....

f) You need a knive if you want to cut that branch.

....

g) Where did you buy your furnitures?

....

3. Comment dirais-tu que :

a) ton pyjama n'est pas sur ton lit.

....

b) ton pantalon préféré est bleu.

....

c) tes bagages sont lourds.

....

d) les nouvelles ne sont pas très bonnes ce matin.

....

EXERCICE 1

a) He needs **an address book.**

b) He needs **stamps.**

c) He needs **a calculator.**

EXERCICE 2

a) He's **an** American actor.

b) Leave your coats in **the** hall.

c) My grandmother is **a** doctor.

d) I have got **a** cousin who lives in York.

EXERCICE 3

a) Can I have stamps?
Can I have a stamp?

b) My friends are teachers.
My friend is a teacher.

c) We saw camels in the desert.
We saw a camel in the desert.

d) Look at the planes in the sky!
Look at the plane in the sky!

44 A / AN / THE

● **L'article indéfini.**

– Au singulier :
a devant un mot commençant par une consonne.
an devant un mot commençant par une voyelle ou un « h » muet *(an animal, an hour).*

Attention !
On dira *a university, a yellow* club car ici le « u » et le « y » se prononçant [ju :], le premier son est donc celui d'une consonne.

– Au pluriel : l'article indéfini disparaît.

Remarque
On met l'article indéfini devant les noms de métiers.

● **L'article défini.**

The : il s'utilise au masculin, au féminin, au neutre, au singulier ou pluriel.

1. C'est la rentrée et Stan fait ses courses. Écris ce dont il a besoin en te reportant au vocabulaire du lexique.

a) He needs ....
....

b) He needs ....
....

c) He needs ....
....

2. Complète les phrases suivantes à l'aide de *a, an* ou *the*.

a) He's .... American actor.

b) Leave your coats in .... hall.

c) My grandmother is .... doctor.

d) I have got .... cousin who lives in York.

3. Mets les phrases suivantes au singulier.

a) Can I have stamps?
....

b) My friends are teachers.
....

c) We saw camels in the desert.
....

d) Look at the planes in the sky!
....

EXERCICE 1

a) I am reading **a** very funny comic strip.

b) I think I need **some** fresh air!

c) My neighbour has **a** very nice garden.

d) Do you need **a** glass?

e) She wants **an** apple.

EXERCICE 2

DÉNOMBRABLES

Vegetables

a potato
an onion
a tomato
a pea
a carrot

Fruits

a banana
an orange
an apple

INDÉNOMBRABLES

Meat

some chicken
some beef
some pork
some lamb
some steak
some veal

Drinks

some orange juice
some water
some milk
some tea
some coffee
some fruit juice

45 DÉNOMBRABLES / INDÉNOMBRABLES

● **Dénombrables.**

On peut compter :
One / an apple, two apples.
One / a flower, two flowers.

– Au singulier, les dénombrables sont précédés de l'article défini ou indéfini ***(the, a, an)***.

– Au pluriel, ils peuvent être précédés de l'article défini ***the*** ou de ***some*** (voir chapitres 44 et 54.)

● **Indénombrables.**

On ne peut pas compter (« du », « de la »).
Les indénombrables sont toujours au singulier.
Ils peuvent être précédés de *some* (voir chapitre 54).
Some rice, some salt.

1. Complète les phrases avec *a, an* ou *some*.

a) I am reading .... very funny comic strip.

b) I think I need .... fresh air!

c) My neighbour has .... very nice garden.

d) Do you need .... glass?

e) She wants .... apple.

2. Classe chaque mot dans la bonne colonne, en ajoutant *a* ou *some*.
potato / onion / chicken / beef / orange juice / water / banana / apple / tomato / pea / pork / milk / tea / carrot / lamb / steak / coffee / veal / fruit juice / orange

DÉNOMBRABLES
Vegetables

....

....

....

....

Fruits

....

....

....

....

INDÉNOMBRABLES
Meat

....

....

....

....

Drinks

....

....

....

....

EXERCICE 1

a) **Whose table is this?**

b) **Whose raincoat is this?**

c) **Whose biscuits are these?**

d) **Whose umbrella is this?**

e) **Whose book is this?**

f) **Whose camera is this?**

EXERCICE 2

a) **Whose** car is in my garage?

b) **Who's** eating all the porridge?

c) Please tell me **who's** on the roof!

d) **Who's** going to wash the dishes today?

e) **Who's** singing?

f) **Whose** glasses are those? Yours?

46 *WHO? / WHOSE?*

● ***Who*** **interroge sur l'identité d'une personne.**

Who is coming to the swimming pool?
Qui vient à la piscine ?

Remarque
Who's est la contraction de *who is.*

● ***Whose*** **interroge sur l'appartenance.**

Whose camera is that?
À qui est cet appareil photo ?

Il se place avant **l'objet** sur lequel porte la question.

● **Attention !**

Whose et *who's* se prononcent de la même façon mais n'ont pas le même sens.

1. Demande à qui appartiennent les objets suivants.

Ex. : (keys) ***Whose keys are these?***

a) (table) ....?

b) (raincoat) ....?

c) (biscuits) ....?

d) (umbrella) ....?

e) (book) ....?

f) (camera) ....?

2. Complète les phrases avec *whose* ou *who's*.

a) .... car is in my garage?

b) .... eating all the porridge?

c) Please tell me .... on the roof!

d) .... going to wash the dishes today?

e) .... singing?

f) .... glasses are those? Yours?

Ta motivation n'est pas la même que celle de tes copains et copines. Elle t'appartient... Alors, fais-en quelque chose!

EXERCICE 1

a) Who's **Daphne's** sister? It's Diana.

b) Who's Cheryl's husband? It's **James**.

c) Who's **Paul's** brother? It's James.

d) Emma is Angelica's **grandmother**.

e) Diana is **Angelica's** cousin.

f) Patty is **Paul's** wife.

EXERCICE 2

a) Where's the dog**'s** food?

b) This is the teacher**'s** pen.

c) Those are my parents**'** suitcases.
(→ Si le nom est au pluriel et se termine par un s*, tu n'as pas besoin d'utiliser* 's *en entier. Mets seulement l'apostrophe.)*

d) Can you go to the chemist**'s** and buy me some aspirin?
(→ Pour parler d'un magasin, on utilise 's*, le mot* shop *est sous-entendu.)*

e) My aunt**'s** house isn't very far.

EXERCICE 3

Dis que :

a) la voiture de tes grands-parents n'est pas neuve.
My grandparents' car isn't new.

b) le mari de Sue est irlandais.
Sue's husband is Irish.

c) tu ne vas jamais chez le boulanger.
I never go to the baker's.

47 FORME POSSESSIVE - *'S*

● **Construction.**

Attention à l'ordre des mots ! possesseur + *'s* + objet possédé

This is Sandra's bedroom.
C'est la chambre de Sandra.

● **Pluriel.**

– Le *'s* disparaît pour les pluriels réguliers.

The teachers' cars.
Les voitures des professeurs.

– Pour les pluriels irréguliers, on met *-'s*.

The children's bags.
Les sacs des enfants.

● **Magasins.**

At the butcher's (shop).
Chez le boucher.

At the chemist's (shop).
Chez le pharmacien.

Shop est sous-entendu.

1. Complète les phrases en observant l'arbre généalogique.

Tim + Emma

Cheryl + James — Paul + Patty

Angelica — Daphne — Diana

a) Who's .... sister?
It's Diana.

b) Who's Cheryl's husband?

It's ....

c) Who's .... brother?
It's James.

d) Emma is Angelica's ....

e) Diana is .... cousin.

f) Patty is .... wife.

2. Complète les phrases à l'aide de l'apostrophe ou de *-'s*.

a) Where's the dog .... food?

b) This is the teacher .... pen.

c) Those are my parents .... suitcases.

d) Can you go to the chemist .... and buy me some aspirin?

e) My aunt .... house isn't very far.

3. Comment dirais-tu que :

a) la voiture de tes grands-parents n'est pas neuve.

....

....

b) le mari de Sue est irlandais.

....

c) tu ne vas jamais chez le boulanger.

....

....

EXERCICE 1

a) What's **your** name? My name's Peter.

b) I have a brother. **His** name's Patrick.

c) This is my sister. **Her** name's Myriam.

d) We don't want to sell **our** house.

e) Where are the children? They're on holiday with **their** parents.

EXERCICE 2

a) This is **my** calendar and that's **yours**.

b) We'll take **our** boots because it's raining.

c) Is **their** new house comfortable?

d) I didn't take his book. I took **hers**.

e) That purse isn't his. It's **mine**.

EXERCICE 3

a) Where is **your** uncle?

b) Is this **their** parents' house?

c) These jeans are Helen's. They're not **yours**!

d) Jim's here and **his** cousins are over there.

e) I'm looking for **my** sister.

LES ADJECTIFS POSSESSIFS

my	mon / ma / mes
your	ton / ta / tes
his / her / its	son / sa / ses
our	notre / nos
your	votre / vos
their	leur / leurs

LES PRONOMS POSSESSIFS

mine
le mien / la mienne,
les miens / les miennes

yours
le tien / la tienne,
les tiens / les tiennes

his / hers / its
le sien / la sienne,
les siens / les siennes

ours
le nôtre / la nôtre / les nôtres

yours
le vôtre / la vôtre / les vôtres

theirs
le leur /la leur / les leurs

48 ADJECTIFS ET PRONOMS POSSESSIFS

● **Les adjectifs possessifs.**

Ils se rapportent à un nom. Ils sont invariables.
My friend / my friends.

● **Les pronoms possessifs.**

Ils remplacent un adjectif possessif + un nom.
It's ***her book****.*
C'est son livre.
It's ***hers****.*
C'est le sien.

● **Attention !**

À la 3e personne du singulier, on choisit l'adjectif et le pronom possessif en fonction du **possesseur** : *his* si le possesseur est **masculin**, *her* ou *hers* si le possesseur est **féminin**, *its* pour le **neutre**.

1. Complète les phrases à l'aide de l'adjectif possessif qui convient.

a) What's .... name? My name's Peter.

b) I have a brother. .... name's Patrick.

c) This is my sister .... name's Myriam.

d) We don't want to sell .... house.

e) Where are the children? They're on holiday with .... parents.

2. Réécris les phrases en corrigeant les erreurs.

a) This is mine calendar and that's your.

....

b) We'll take ours boots because it's raining.

....

c) Is theirs new house comfortable?

....

d) I didn't take his book. I took her.

....

e) That purse isn't his. It's my.

....

3. Choisis la bonne réponse et complète les phrases.

a) Where is .... uncle? (your / mine / hers)

b) Is this .... parents' house? (yours / their /its)

c) These jeans are Helen's. They're not ....! (your / yours / our)

d) Jim's here and .... cousins are over there. (her / mine / his)

e) I'm looking for .... sister. (my / theirs / yours)

EXERCICE 1

a) **I always do my homework.**

b) **I sometimes play darts**

c) **I never drive a car.**

d) **I often get up late.**

e) **I am sometimes sad.**

EXERCICE 2

a) Do you play on your computer? (never)
No, I never play on my computer.

b) How often does your family go on holiday? (often)
My family often goes on holiday.

c) Are you often sick? (rarely)
No, I'm rarely sick.

d) Does your aunt visit you? (sometimes)
Yes, my aunt sometimes visits me/us.

EXERCICE 3

a) **How often do you take piano lessons?**
I take piano lessons twice a week.

b) **How often do you use your mobile phone?**
I use my mobile phone every day.

c) **How often are you late?**
I am never late.

Attention à la traduction de *How often*? en français !

How often do you go to the swimming pool?

Tous les combien vas-tu à la piscine ?

LES MARQUEURS DE TEMPS

once a week : une fois par semaine

twice a month : deux fois par mois

four times a year : quatre fois par an

on Mondays : tous les lundis

at weekends : tous les week-ends

→ Les marqueurs de temps se placent en fin de phrase.

49 ADVERBES DE FRÉQUENCE

Emploi.

Ils servent à parler de la fréquence d'une action au présent simple.
Does she always watch the news?

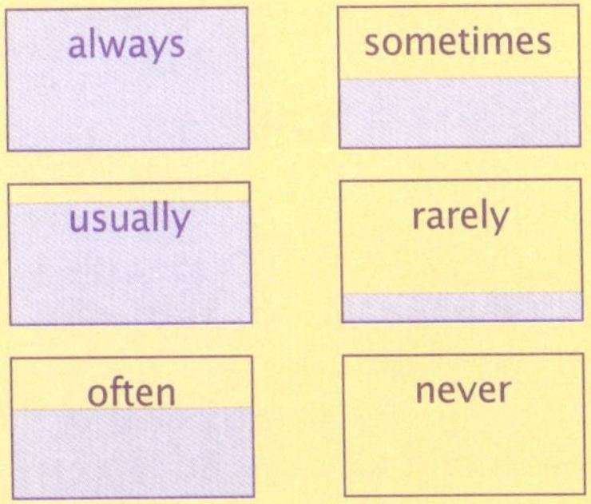

Question.

How often? permet de poser une question sur la fréquence.
How often do you drive?

1. Fais des phrases à l'aide des informations données dans le tableau.

Ex. : ***I usually brush my teeth after lunch.***

	sometimes	usually	always	often	never
brush my teeth after lunch		x			
a) **do my homework**			x		
b) **play darts**	x				
c) **drive a car**					x
d) **get up late**				x	
e) **be sad**	x				

a) ....

b) ....

c) ....

d) ....

e) ....

2. Réponds aux questions de Peter à l'aide des adverbes entre parenthèses.

Ex. : How often do you take a shower? (usually)
I usually take a shower.

a) Do you play on your computer? (never)

No, ...

b) How often does your family go on holiday? (often)

My family ....

c) Are you often sick? (rarely)

No, I ....

d) Does your aunt visit you? (sometimes)

Yes, ...

3. Trouve les questions correspondant aux réponses. Fais des phrases avec *How often?*

Ex. : ***How often do you go to the theatre?***
I sometimes go to the theatre.

a) ....
I take piano lessons twice a week.

b) ....
I use my mobile phone every day.

c) ....
I am never late.

EXERCICE 1

a) Terry / know / the Smiths
How long has Terry known the Smiths?

b) Paul and Jane / live / in London
How long have Paul and Jane lived in London?

c) he / be / an engineer
How long has he been an engineer?

EXERCICE 2

a) do / eat / often /fish / how / you / ?
How often do you eat fish?

b) you / have / how / rabbits / long / had / ?
How long have you had rabbits?

c) Sydney / it / rain / how / does / often / in / ?
How often does it rain in Sydney?

EXERCICE 3

a) How often **does** the phone **ring**?

b) How long **have** they **kept** the secret?

c) How often **do** you **go** to the zoo?

d) How long **has** your cousin **had** a fever?

EXERCICE 4

Demande à Nancy :

a) Depuis combien de temps es-tu au lit ?
How long have you been in bed?
(➜ Attention, le présent simple en français se traduit par un present perfect *en anglais lorsque l'on pose une question introduite par* How long?*)*

b) Tous les combien vas-tu à la piscine ?
How often do you go to the swimming pool?

50 HOW LONG? / HOW OFTEN?

● ***How long? + present perfect.***

Pour poser une question sur la durée d'une action qui se poursuit dans le présent.
How long has Susie known Paul?
Depuis combien de temps Susie connaît-elle Paul ?

● ***How often?* + présent simple.**

– Pour poser une question sur la fréquence d'une action :
How often do you buy magazines?
Tous les combien achètes-tu un magazine ?

– Pour répondre avec un adverbe de fréquence *(sometimes, usually, often, always, never)*, revois le chapitre 49.

1. Pose des questions au *present perfect + How long?* à l'aide des mots proposés.

a) Terry / know / the Smiths

....

b) Paul and Jane / live / in London

....

c) he / be / an engineer

....

2. Remets les mots dans le bon ordre pour poser des questions avec *How long?* ou *How often?*

a) do / eat / often / fish / how / you / ?

....?

b) you / have / how / rabbits / long / had / ?

....?

c) Sydney / it / rain / how / does / often / in / ?

....?

3. Complète les phrases à l'aide des verbes entre parenthèses conjugués au présent simple ou au *present perfect*.

a) How often .... the phone .... (ring)?

b) How long .... they .... (keep) the secret?

c) How often .... you .... (go) to the zoo?

d) How long .... your cousin .... (have) a fever?

4. Pose les questions suivantes à Nancy.

a) Depuis combien de temps es-tu au lit ?

....?

b) Tous les combien vas-tu à la piscine ?

....?

EXERCICE 1

a) **How many** people will you invite?

b) **How many** books did you read during your holidays?

c) **How much** is that tennis racket?

d) **How much** milk do we need?

e) **How much** cheese would you like?

f) **How many** doctors are there in your town?

EXERCICE 2

a) **How many pupils are there in the classroom?**
There are 20 pupils in the classroom.

b) **How many brothers and sisters have they got?**
They have got six brothers and sisters.

c) **How many dangerous lions can you see in the street?**
I can see six dangerous lions in the street!

d) **How much does it cost?**
It costs £300.

e) **How much does he want to spend ?**
He wants to spend only $6!

EXERCICE 3

Demande

a) combien coûte le menu.
How much is the menu? / How much does the menu cost?

b) combien il y a de journaux dans le sac de Ben.
How many newspapers are there in Ben's bag?

c) combien il y a de joueurs dans une équipe de rugby.
How many players are there in a rugby team?

d) combien d'argent veut Bob.
How much money does Bob want?

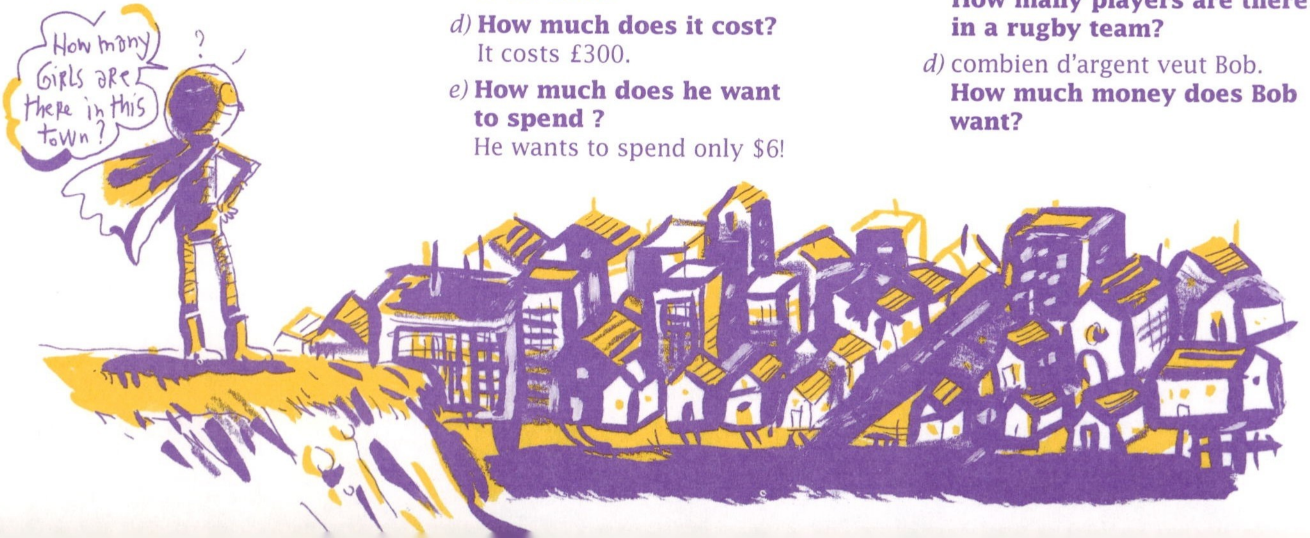

51 HOW MUCH? / HOW MANY?

How much? et *How many?* servent à interroger sur la quantité : « combien », « combien de ».

- **Indénombrables :** ***how much*** **+ singulier.**

How much money have we got?
Combien d'argent avons-nous ?

- **Dénombrables :** ***how many*** **+ pluriel .**

How many days did you stay in Holland?
Combien de jours es-tu resté en Hollande ?

Remarque
How much sert aussi à demander un prix.
How much do these books cost?
Combien coûtent ces livres ?
How much is this pen?
Combien coûte ce stylo ?

1. *How much* ou *how many*?

a) .... people will you invite?

b) .... books did you read during your holidays?

c) .... is that tennis racket?

d) .... milk do we need?

e) .... cheese would you like?

f) .... doctors are there in your town?

2. Trouve la question pour chacune des réponses données, comme dans l'exemple.

Ex. : ***How much are those pens?***
Those pens are 55 pence each.

a) ....?
There are 20 pupils in the classroom.

b) ....?
They have got six brothers and sisters.

c) ....?
I can see six dangerous lions in the street!

d) ....?
It costs £300.

e) ....?
He wants to spend only $6!

3. Comment demanderais-tu ?

a) Combien coûte le menu ?

....?

b) Combien il y a de journaux dans le sac de Ben ?

....?

c) Combien il y a de joueurs dans une équipe de rugby ?

....?

d) Combien d'argent veut Bob ?

....?

EXERCICE 1

a) Jimmy invited **many** people!

b) There isn't **much** food!

c) There aren't **many** drinks!

d) There aren't **many** sandwiches!

e) There aren't **many** chairs!

f) There isn't **much** fruit juice!

EXERCICE 2

Dis que:

a) tu as beaucoup de travail.
I have a lot of work. /
I have plenty of work.

b) tu n'as pas beaucoup de temps.
I haven't got much time. /
I haven't got a lot of time.

c) il n'y a pas beaucoup de pièces dans ta maison.
There aren't many rooms in my house.

Si tu as beaucoup de bonnes notes, continue ainsi!
Si tu as beaucoup de mauvaises notes, prends confiance en toi et travaille un peu plus!

52 MUCH / MANY / A LOT OF / PLENTY OF

● **Poser une question sur la quantité (« beaucoup de »).**

– ***much*** + indénombrables.
Do you drink much coke?
Bois-tu beaucoup de coca ?

– ***many*** + dénombrables.
Did you take many photographs?
Avez-vous pris beaucoup de photos?

● **Dire que l'on a « beaucoup de ».**

– ***a lot of / lots of / plenty of*** + dénombrables ou indénombrables.

– ***many*** + dénombrables.
I have many / a lot of / lots of / plenty of problems.
J'ai beaucoup de problèmes.

● **Dire que l'on n'a « pas beaucoup de ».**

– ***not much*** + indénombrables.
We haven't got much money.
Nous n'avons pas beaucoup d'argent.

– ***not many*** + dénombrables.
There aren't many trains today.
Il n'y a pas beaucoup de trains aujourd'hui.

1. La fête d'anniversaire de James a été mal organisée. Commente le dessin, en utilisant *much* ou *many*.

a) James invited .... people!

b) There isn't .... food!

c) There aren't .... drinks!

d) There aren't .... sandwiches!

e) There aren't .... chairs!

f) There isn't .... fruit juice!

2. Dis que :

a) tu as beaucoup de travail.

....

....

b) tu n'as pas beaucoup de temps.

....

....

c) n'y a pas beaucoup de pièces dans ta maison.

....

....

Deux solutions sont possibles pour a) et b).

EXERCICE 1

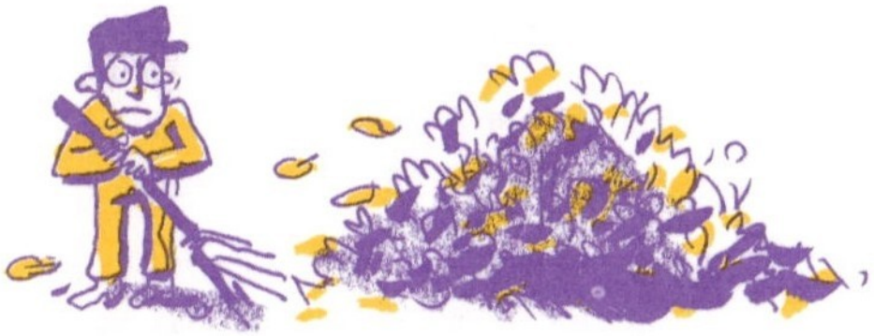

a) **too much work.**

b) **too many planes.**

c) **too difficult.**

EXERCICE 2

a) There's **too much** noise. I can't hear you.

b) (On the phone) The line is **too** bad. Can you repeat?

c) You're **too** stupid to understand!

d) Don't take **too many** clothes!

e) That man drinks **too much** beer.

f) There's **too much** traffic. We'll be late!

g) Our teacher gives us **too many** exercises to do.

EXERCICE 3

Dis que :

a) le café est trop fort.
The coffee is too strong.

b) la gare est trop loin.
The station is too far.

c) ton pantalon est trop court.
My trousers are too short.

53

TOO / TOO MUCH / TOO MANY

● ***Too* + adjectif ou adverbe**

signifie « trop ».
I'm too busy. I can't go out.
Je suis trop occupé. Je ne peux pas sortir.

● ***Too much* + indénombrable**

signifie « trop de ».
They have too much work.
Ils ont trop de travail.

● ***Too many* + dénombrable**

signifie « trop de ».
She has too many video games.
Elle a trop de jeux vidéo.

1. Quel est le problème ? Fais des phrases à l'aide de *too much*, *too many*, *too* et un adjectif ou un nom approprié. Utilise les mots suivants : *work / difficult / planes*.

Ex. : ***too hot.***

a) ....

b) ....

c) ....

2. Complète les phrases à l'aide de *too*, *too much* ou *too many*.

a) There's .... noise. I can't hear you.

b) (On the phone) The line is .... bad. Can you repeat?

c) You're .... stupid to understand!

d) Don't take .... clothes!

e) That man drinks .... beer.

f) There's .... traffic. We'll be late!

g) Our teacher gives us .... exercises to do.

3. Dis que :

a) le café est trop fort.

....

b) la gare est trop loin.

....

c) ton pantalon est trop court.

....

EXERCICE 1

a) We saw **some** horses in the park.

b) Are there **any** elephants in the jungle?

c) Have you got **any** homework to do?

d) My neighbours haven't got **any** children.

e) Would you like **some** more apple pie?

EXERCICE 2

a) We didn't buy any biscuits.
We bought no biscuits.

b) There weren't any clouds in the sky.
There were no clouds in the sky.

c) He doesn't have any exercises to do.
He has no exercises to do.

d) There aren't any flowers.
There are no flowers.

e) We won't buy any wine.
We'll buy no wine.

EXERCICE 3

a) **1** : There aren't some photos on the TV.
2 : There are no photos on the TV.

b) **1** : Is there some water?
2 : Is there any water?

c) **1** : I didn't buy any eggs.
2 : I didn't buy no eggs.

d) **1** : Are there no farms around here?
2 : Are there any farms around here?

e) **1** : I don't want some cereals, thank you.
2 : I don't want any cereals, thank you.

54 SOME / ANY / NO

Some et *any* désignent une quantité indéfinie : «du», «de la», « des ».

- **Affirmation : *some*.**

I have some money.
J'ai de l'argent.

- **Question : *any*.**

Do you have any money?
As-tu de l'argent ?

Remarque
Pour proposer ou offrir quelque chose, on emploie ***some*** à la forme interrogative.
Would you like some cheese?

- **Négation.**

– ***Any*** avec un verbe à la forme négative.
There aren't any bananas.
Il n'y a pas de bananes.
– ***No*** avec un verbe à la forme affirmative.
There are no eggs.
Il n'y a pas d'œufs.

1. Complète à l'aide de *some* ou *any*.

a) We saw .... horses in the park.

b) Are there .... elephants in the jungle?

c) Have you got .... homework to do?

d) My neighbours haven't got

.... children.

e) Would you like .... more apple pie?

2. Réécris les phrases en utilisant *no*.

Ex. : There aren't any computers.
There are no computers.

a) We didn't buy any biscuits.

....

b) There weren't any clouds in the sky.

....

c) He doesn't have any exercises to do.

....

d) There aren't any flowers.

....

e) We won't buy any wine.

....

3. 1 ou 2 ? Souligne la phrase correcte.

a) **1** : There aren't some photos on the TV.
2 : There are no photos on the TV.

b) **1** : Is there some water?
2 : Is there any water?

c) **1** : I didn't buy any eggs.
2 : I didn't buy no eggs.

d) **1** : Are there no farms around here?
2 : Are there any farms around here?

e) **1** : I don't want some cereals, thank you.
2 : I don't want any cereals, thank you.

EXERCICE 1

a) She lives **somewhere** in New Jersey.

b) Is there **anything** on TV tonight?

c) Does **anyone** want ice-cream?

d) I'd like **something** to drink.

EXERCICE 2

a) I can't see anybody.
I can see nobody.

b) They don't drink anything.
They drink nothing.

c) She didn't tell anybody.
She told nobody.

Rappel

somewhere : quelque part
someone / somebody : quelqu'un
something : quelque chose

nowhere + verbe à la forme affirmative *anywhere* + verbe à la forme négative	nulle part
no one / nobody + verbe à la forme affirmative *anyone / anybody* + verbe à la forme négative	personne
nothing + verbe à la forme affirmative *anything* + verbe à la forme négative	rien

55 COMPOSÉS DE *SOME, ANY, NO*

● Composés de *some* :

– pour parler d'une chose indéfinie : *something* ;
– pour parler d'un lieu indéfini : *somewhere* ;
– pour parler d'une personne indéfinie : *somebody / someone.*

I saw somebody.
J'ai vu quelqu'un.

● Composés de *any* :

– pour poser une question : *anything, anywhere, anybody / anyone.*
– pour donner un sens négatif + verbe à la forme négative

Did you see anyone? I didn't see anybody.
As-tu vu quelqu'un? Je n'ai vu personne.

● Composés de *no* :

– pour donner un sens négatif + verbe à la forme affirmative : *nothing, nowhere, nobody, no one.*

I saw nobody.
Je n'ai vu personne.

1. Complète les phrases à l'aide des mots suivants : *something / anywhere / somewhere / anyone / anything.*

a) She lives .... in New Jersey.

b) Is there .... on TV tonight ?

c) Does .... want ice cream?

d) I'd like .... to drink.

2. Transforme les phrases comme dans l'exemple.

Ex. : We didn't go anywhere last night.
We went nowhere last night.

a) I can't see anybody.

....

b) They don't drink anything.

....

c) She didn't tell anybody.

....

Retiens bien ce chapitre :
il t'aidera à en comprendre
beaucoup d'autres.

VOCABULAIRE

at school, at home : à l'école, à la maison
at the baker's : chez le boulanger, à la boulangerie
on television : à la télévision
on the bus : dans le bus
on the left of... : à gauche de...
on the right of... : à droite de...

the baker's : le boulanger
the bank : la banque
the book shop : le libraire
the butcher's : le boucher
the chemist's : le pharmacien
the library : la bibliothèque
the post-office : la poste
the supermarket : le supermarché
the swimming pool : la piscine
the University : l'université

EXERCICE 1

a) The news paper kiosk is **next to** the cinema.

b) The post-office is **opposite** the cinema and **behind** the butcher's.

c) The baker's is **between** the supermarket and the swimming-pool.

EXERCICE 2

B	G	R	D	A	B	O	V	E	A	Y	U
E	E	L	I	P	M	P	J	C	K	L	N
S	T	W	D	J	D	P	R	Z	T	F	D
I	W	I	L	N	O	O	F	K	M	I	E
D	B	E	L	O	W	S	A	O	T	I	R
E	G	G	E	V	T	I	P	U	K	N	E
A	R	G	F	O	N	T	O	V	I	U	F
B	C	F	K	L	B	E	T	W	E	E	N

56 PRÉPOSITIONS DE LIEU

● Emploi.

Ces prépositions aident à localiser.

above	au-dessus de
at	à
behind	derrière
below	au-dessous de
beside	à côté de
between	entre
in	dans
in front of	devant
near	près de
next to	à côté de
on	sur
opposite	en face de
under	sous

The library is opposite the post-office, next to the flowershop.
La bibliothèque est en face de la poste, à côté du fleuriste.

1. Regarde le plan de la ville. Complète les phrases à l'aide des propositions suivantes : *opposite - between - next to - behind.*

a) The news paper kiosk is .... the cinema.

b) The post-office is ....

the cinema and .... the butcher's.

c) The baker's is .... the supermarket and the swimming-pool.

2. Cherche et souligne les six prépositions cachées dans la grille. Elles se trouvent dans les lignes à l'horizontale ou à la verticale, de droite à gauche. La première a déjà été encadrée pour toi.

B	G	R	D	[A	B	O	V	E]	A	Y	U
E	E	I	L	I	M	P	J	C	K	L	N
S	T	W	D	J	D	P	R	Z	T	F	D
I	W	I	L	N	O	O	F	K	M	I	E
D	B	E	L	O	W	S	A	O	T	I	R
E	G	G	E	V	T	I	P	U	K	N	E
A	R	G	F	O	N	T	O	V	I	U	F
B	C	F	K	L	B	E	T	W	E	E	N

QUELQUES VERBES DE MOUVEMENT

to climb : escalader
to come : venir
to go : aller
to jump : sauter
to run : courir
to swim : nager
to throw : lancer, jeter
to walk : marcher

EXERCICE 1

You leave from your home. Walk to the library. Turn right on King street, go across the bridge. Walk through the park, to the Main Fountain and up Ashley street. My building is on your right, between the baker's and the bank.

EXERCICE 2

a) I threw it **into** the paper bin.

b) Mark drove **from** Southampton **to** London.

c) He needed medicines, so she ran **to** the chemist's.

d) She threw the ball **through** the window.

e) Let's get **out of** the house and go for a walk.

f) She ran **up** the stairs and now she is tired.

g) Can you jump **over** a chair?

57 PRÉPOSITIONS DE MOUVEMENT

● **Emploi.**

Ces prépositions indiquent le déplacement. Elles se placent après les verbes de mouvement.

To run ***to*** : en direction de
To go ***into*** : dans + idée de déplacement
To leave ***from*** : de (la provenance)
To go ***out of*** : sortir de

across *the bridge* : de l'autre côté...
along *the road* : le long...
down *the stairs* : vers le bas...
over *the ocean...* : au-dessus de, par dessus...
through *the wall* : à travers...
up *the mountain* : vers le haut...

1. D'après ces indications, dessine le chemin que suit Peter pour aller chez son amie, Jane.

You leave from your home. Walk to the library. Turn right on King street, go across the bridge. Walk through the park, to the Main Fountain and up Ashley street. My building is on your right, between the baker's and the bank.

2. Complète les phrases par la préposition de mouvement qui convient : *from – to – up – over – into – through – to – out of*.

a) I threw it .... the paper bin.

b) Mark drove .... Southampton .... London.

c) She threw the ball .... the window.

d) He needed medicines, so she ran .... the chemist's.

e) Let's get .... the house and go for a walk.

f) She ran .... the stairs and now she is tired.

g) Can you jump .... a chair?

EXERCICE 1

I get up **at** 7 o'clock **in** the morning, then I have breakfast.
I usually go to work **by** car. I start work **at** eight o'clock. **In** the morning, I am always very busy. I usually make a lot of phone calls **before** lunch. **On** Fridays, I don't work, so I stay at home.

EXERCICE 2

a) Caterina lit des livres en italien.
Caterina reads books in Italian.

b) Ce matin, j'ai acheté une robe pour ma sœur.
This morning, I bought a dress for my sister.

c) Est-ce que tu as offert un cadeau à ton père hier ?
Did you give a present to your father yesterday?

d) Je veux venir avec toi.
I want to come with you.

EXERCICE 3

a) The Fergusons drink tea **at quarter past five**.

b) Students go to school **from twenty past eight to quarter to four**.

c) The movie begins **at quarter to eleven**.

L'HEURE

It's quarter past eleven.

It's half past seven.

It's quarter to eight.

It's twenty five to four.

58 AUTRES PRÉPOSITIONS

● **Temps.**

after *dinner* : après le dîner
at *five o'clock* : à 5h
before *lunch* : avant le déjeuner
from *9* ***to*** *10* : de 9h à 10h
in *the morning* : le matin
on *Fridays* : le vendredi
ten ***past*** *six* : 6h 10
five ***to*** *seven* : 7h moins 5

● **Destination.**

for *you* : pour toi
to *you* : à toi

● **Accompagnement.**

with *you* : avec toi

● **Moyen.**

by *car* : en voiture
with *the key* : avec la clé
in *Arabic* : en arabe

1. Complète l'emploi du temps de Jane à l'aide de la préposition qui convient.

I get up .... 7 o'clock .... the morning, then I have breakfast. I usually go to work .... car. I start work .... eight o'clock. .... the morning, I am always very busy. I usually make a lot of phone calls .... lunch. .... Fridays, I don't work, so I stay at home.

2. Comment dirais-tu ces phrases en anglais :

a) Caterina lit des livres en italien.

....

b) J'ai acheté une robe pour ma sœur.

....

c) Est-ce que tu as offert un cadeau à ton père hier ?

....

d) Je veux venir avec toi.

....

3. Complète les phrases à l'aide de la préposition qui convient et de l'heure affichée.
at – from – to

a) The Fergusons drink tea ....

....

b) Students go to school ....

....

....

....

c) The movie begins

....

....

VOCABULAIRE

one : un
two : deux
three : trois
four : quatre
five : cinq
six : six
seven : sept
eight : huit
nine : neuf
ten : dix
eleven : onze
twelve : douze

Nombres terminés en *-een* :

*thir**teen*** : treize
*four**teen*** : quatorze
*fif**teen*** : quinze
*six**teen*** : seize
*seven**teen*** : dix-sept
*eigh**teen*** : dix-huit
*nine**teen*** : dix-neuf

Nombres terminés en *-y* :

*twent**y*** : vingt
*thirt**y*** : trente
*fort**y*** : quarante
*fift**y*** : cinquante
*sixt**y*** : soixante
*sevent**y*** : soixante-dix
*eight**y*** : quatre-vingt
*ninet**y*** : quatre-vingt-dix

a / one hundred : cent
a / one thousand : mille
a / one million : un million

EXERCICE 1

a) 239.095.873
two three nine oh nine five eight seven three

b) 003.55.16.32
double oh three double five one six three two

c) 38.12.66.34
three eight one two double six three four

d) 55.33.01.62
double five double three oh one six two

e) 985.432.75
nine eight five four three two seven five

EXERCICE 2

a) 1874 **eighteen seventy four**
b) 1982 **nineteen eighty two**
c) 1623 **sixteen twenty three**
d) 1794 **seventeen ninety four**
e) 1932 **nineteen thirty two**

EXERCICE 3

14 • — • fourteen
81 • — • eighty-one
25 • — • twenty-five
13 • — • thirteen
67 • — • sixty-seven
30 • — • thirty
40 • — • forty

59 NOMBRES CARDINAUX

Les nombres cardinaux s'utilisent

- **pour compter.**

Attention ! Ne confonds pas :

	-een		**-y**
13	*thirt**een***	30	*thirt**y***
14	*fourt**een***	40	*fort**y***
15	*fift**een***	50	*fift**y***
16	*sixt**een***	60	*sixt**y***
17	*sevent**een***	70	*sevent**y***
18	*eight**een***	80	*eight**y***
19	*ninet**een***	90	*ninet**y***

- **pour indiquer l'âge, l'année.**

I'm thirteen (13) years old.
J'ai 13 ans.
I was born in nineteen eighty-six (1986).
Je suis né(e) en 1986.

Remarque
Pour lire les années, on décompose le nombre en deux parties.

- **pour donner un numéro de téléphone.**

Les chiffres sont lus séparément. Le 0 se dit « oh », le même chiffre répété deux fois se lit *double...* (99 = *double nine*).

1. Écris les numéros de téléphone en toutes lettres.

a) 239.095.873

....

b) 003.55.16.32

....

c) 38.12.66.34

....

d) 55.33.01.62

....

e) 985.432.75

....

2. Écris les années en toutes lettres.

a) 1874 ....

b) 1982 ....

c) 1623 ....

d) 1794 ....

e) 1932 ....

3. Relie les chiffres avec leur équivalent en lettres.

14 ▪	▪ thirty
81 ▪	▪ sixty-seven
25 ▪	▪ forty
13 ▪	▪ fourteen
67 ▪	▪ eighty-one
30 ▪	▪ thirteen
40 ▪	▪ twenty-five

VOCABULAIRE

first : premier
second : second
third : troisième
fourth : quatrième
fifth : cinquième
sixth : sixième
seventh : septième
eighth : huitième
ninth : neuvième
tenth : dixième
eleventh : onzième
twelfth : douzième
thirteenth : treizième
fourteenth : quatorzième
fifteenth : quinzième
sixteenth : seizième
seventeenth : dix-septième
eigteenth : dix-huitième
nineteenth : dix-neuvième
twentieth : vingtième
twenty-first : vingt et unième
thirtieth : trentième
fortieth : quarantième
fiftieth : cinquantième
sixtieth : soixantième
seventieth : soixante-dixième
eightieth : quatre-vingtième
ninetieth : quatre-vingt-dixième

EXERCICE 1

a) 3rd, 5th, **7th, 9th, 11th, 13th, 15th**

b) 10th, 20th, **30th, 40th, 50th, 60th, 70th**

EXERCICE 2

a) **Stan was fourth (4th).**

b) **Kathy was fifth (5th)**

c) **Joe was first (1st).**

d) **David was second (2nd).**

EXERCICE 3

a) 30.07
– **The thirtieth of July**
– **July thirtieth**

b) 23.12
– **The twenty-third of December**
– **December twenty-third**

Quel résultat veux-tu pour la prochaine interrogation?

Écris le ici ☐ ...
et fais tout pour l'obtenir!

60 NOMBRES ORDINAUX

● **Construction.**

Ils se construisent à partir des nombres cardinaux auxquels on ajoute *-th*.

four quatre — *the fourth* le quatrième

● **Attention !**

– aux exceptions :

one — *first*
two — *second*
three — *third*

– aux modifications orthographiques :
ninth, twelfth, twentieth, thirtieth...

● **Emploi.**

Ils s'utilisent pour indiquer un **ordre**, un **classement** (le premier, le second, etc.) ou pour dire la **date**.
November 12th ou *the 12th of November.*

1. Trouve les cinq nombres qui forment une suite logique, comme dans l'exemple.

Ex. : 12th, 14th, 16th, ***18th, 20th, 22nd, 24th, 26th***

a) 3rd, 5th, 7th, ...

....

b) 10th, 20th, ...

....

2. Classe Jerry et ses camarades en fonction de leurs notes au devoir de mathématiques.

Ex. : ***Jerry was third (3rd).***

a) ....

b) ....

c) ....

d) ....

3. Écris les dates en toutes lettres, des deux façons possibles.

a) 30.07

– ....

– ....

b) 23.12

– ....

– ....

> **Remarque**
> En abrégé, on écrit le chiffre et les deux dernières lettres du mot (*1st, 2nd, 3rd...*).

ANNEXES

1 PRINCIPAUX VERBES IRRÉGULIERS

BASE VERBALE	PRÉTÉRIT	PARTICIPE PASSÉ	FRANÇAIS
Be	Was / were	Been	Être
Begin	Began	Begun	Commencer
Break	Broke	Broken	Casser
Bring	Brought	Brought	Apporter
Build	Built	Built	Construire
Burn	Burnt (US : burned)	Burnt (US : burned)	Brûler
Buy	Bought	Bought	Acheter
Catch	Caught	Caught	Attraper
Choose	Chose	Chosen	Choisir
Come	Came	Come	Venir
Cost	Cost	Cost	Coûter
Cut	Cut	Cut	Couper
Do	Did	Done	Faire
Draw	Drew	Drawn	Dessiner / tirer
Drink	Drank	Drunk	Boire
Drive	Drove	Driven	Conduire
Eat	Ate	Eaten	Manger
Fall	Fell	Fallen	Tomber
Feed	Fed	Fed	Nourrir
Feel	Felt	Felt	Sentir, se sentir

Find	Found	Found	Trouver
Forget	Forgot	Forgotten	Oublier
Get	Got	Got (US : gotten)	Obtenir, devenir
Give	Gave	Given	Donner
Go	Went	Gone	Aller
Have	Had	Had	Avoir
Hear	Heard	Heard	Entendre
Keep	Kept	Kept	Garder
Know	Knew	Known	Savoir, connaître
Learn	Learnt (US : learned)	Learnt (US : learned)	Apprendre
Leave	Left	Left	Partir, laisser, quitter,
Lend	Lent	Lent	Prêter
Lose	Lost	Lost	Perdre
Make	Made	Made	Faire, fabriquer
Meet	Met	Met	Rencontrer
Pay	Paid	Paid	Payer
Put	Put	Put	Mettre
Read	Read	Read	Lire
Ride	Rode	Ridden	Aller (à vélo, à cheval, à moto...)
Ring	Rang	Rung	Sonner
Run	Ran	Run	Courir
Say	Said	Said	Dire
See	Saw	Seen	Voir
Sell	Sold	Sold	Vendre
Send	Sent	Sent	Envoyer
Shut	Shut	Shut	Fermer
Sing	Sang	Sung	Chanter

BASE VERBALE	PASSÉ (PRÉTÉRIT)	PARTICIPE PASSÉ	FRANÇAIS
Sit	Sat	Sat	S'asseoir, être assis
Sleep	Slept	Slept	Dormir
Speak	Spoke	Spoken	Parler
Spend	Spent	Spent	Dépenser, passer du temps
Sweep	Swept	Swept	Balayer
Swim	Swam	Swum	Nager
Take	Took	Taken	Prendre
Teach	Taught	Taught	Enseigner
Tell	Told	Told	Dire, raconter
Think	Thought	Thought	Penser
Understand	Understood	Understood	Comprendre
Wake	Woke (US : waked)	Woken (US : waked)	Se réveiller, s'éveiller
Wear	Wore	Worn	Porter un vêtement
Write	Wrote	Written	Écrire

2 PAYS ET NATIONALITÉS

PAYS	NATIONALITÉS	NOMS DES HABITANTS
Algeria	Algerian	Algerian(s)
Argentina	Argentinian	Argentine(s)
Australia	Australian	Australian(s)
Austria	Austrian	Austrian(s)
Belgium	Belgian	Belgian(s)
Bulgaria	Bulgarian	Bulgar(s)
Cambodia	Cambodian	Cambodian(s)
Cameroon	Cameroonian	Cameroonian(s)
Canada	Canadian	Canadian(s)
China	Chinese	Chinese
Congo (The)	Congolese	Congolese
Czech Republic (The)	Czech	Czech(s)
Denmark	Danish	Dane(s)
England	English	English (wo)man/ the English
Finland	Finnish	Finn(s)
France	French	French (wo)man/ the French
Germany	German	German(s)
Ghana	Ghanaian	Ghanaian(s)
Great Britain	British	Briton(s)/ the British
Greece	Greek	Greek(s)

PAYS	NATIONALITÉS	NOMS DES HABITANTS
Hungary	Hungarian	Hungarian(s)
Iceland	Icelandic	Icelander(s)
India	Indian	Indian(s)
Iraq	Iraqi	Iraqi(s)
Ireland	Irish	Irish (wo)man/ the Irish
Italy	Italian	Italian(s)
Japan	Japanese	Japanese
Laos	Laotian	Laotian(s)
Malta	Maltese	Maltese
Morocco	Moroccan	Moroccan(s)
Netherlands (The)	Dutch	Dutch (wo)man/ the Dutch
Norway	Norwegian	Norwegian(s)
Poland	Polish	Pole(s)
Portugal	Portuguese	Portuguese
Russia	Russian	Russian(s)
Scandinavia	Scandinavian	Scandinavian(s)
Scotland	Scottish	Scots (wo)man/ the Scots
Spain	Spanish	Spaniard(s)
Sweden	Swedish	Swede(s)
Switzerland	Swiss	Swiss
Tunisia	Tunisian	Tunisian(s)
Turkey	Turkish	Turk(s)
USA (The)	American	American(s)
Wales	Welsh	Welsh (wo)man/the Welsh

LEXIQUE

LEXIQUE

A

actor	acteur
address book	carnet d'adresses
afraid	apeuré
agree with (v)	être d'accord avec
always	toujours
ambitious	ambitieux
angry	en colère
answer phone	répondeur (téléphonique)
apple	pomme
April	avril
armchair	fauteuil
around	autour de
arrive (v)	arriver
attic	grenier
August	août
aunt	tante
awful	terrible, horrible, épouvantable

B

baby	bébé
bad	mauvais
bag	sac
baker	boulanger
balcony	balcon
banana	banane
bathroom	salle de bains
beach	plage
beautiful	beau, belle
bedroom	chambre
beef	bœuf
beer	bière
believe (v)	croire
bell	sonnette
big	1. gros 2. grand
bike	vélo
biscuits	des biscuits
book	livre
boot	botte
boring	ennuyeux
borrow (v)	emprunter
bottle	bouteille
box	boîte
branch	branche
break (v)	casser
bridge	pont
brother	frère
brush (v)	brosser
brush one's teeth	*se laver les dents*
building	immeuble
burn (v)	brûler
busy	occupé
butcher	boucher
butterfly	papillon
buy (v)	acheter

C

calculator	calculatrice
calendar	calendrier
call (v)	appeler
camel	chameau
camera	appareil photo
carpet	tapis, moquette
carrot	carotte
carry (v)	porter
catch (v)	attrapper
CD player	lecteur de CD
cellar	cave
chair	chaise
cheap	bon marché
chess	jeu d'échecs
chicken	poulet
church	église
circle (v)	entourer
clean	propre
clean (v)	nettoyer
clever	intelligent
climb (v)	grimper, escalader
clothes	vêtements
cloud	nuage
coat	manteau
coffee	café
coin	pièce (de monnaie)
cold	1. rhume 2. froid *(adjectif)*
comb (v)	se peigner
comfortable	confortable
comic strip	bande dessinée
complain (v)	se plaindre

computer	ordinateur
cook (v)	cuisiner
copybook	cahier
country	1. pays 2. campagne
cousin	cousin
crazy	fou
cross out (v)	barrer
crosswords	mots croisés
cruel	cruel
cry (v)	pleurer
cut (v)	couper
cycle (v)	faire du vélo

D

dance (v)	danser
dangerous	dangereux
dark	sombre
dark-haired	brun
darts	fléchettes
daughter	fille
day	jour
the day before yesterday	*avant-hier*
December	décembre
deep	profond
deliver (v)	livrer
department store	grand magasin
desk	bureau
dining room	salle à manger
dirty	sale
disappointed	déçu
draw (v)	1. dessiner 2. tirer
dress	robe
drink (v)	boire
drink	boisson
drive (v)	conduire
dust (v)	épousseter

E

early	tôt
eat (v)	manger
egg	œuf
end (v)	finir, se terminer
engineer	ingénieur
enjoy (v)	apprécier, bien aimer
enjoy oneself	*s'amuser*
envelope	enveloppe
eraser (US) / rubber (GB)	gomme
every	tous les, chaque
expensive	cher

F

far	loin
farm	ferme
fast	rapide
father	père
favourite	préféré, favori
February	février
feed (v)	nourrir, donner à manger
feel (v)	sentir, se sentir
fever	fièvre
fight (v)	se battre
fine	bien
fireplace	âtre
fireman (firemen)	pompier(s)
fish (v)	pêcher
first floor	premier étage
first name	prénom
flat	appartement
flower	fleur
fly (v)	voler, prendre l'avion
food	nourriture
foot (feet)	pied(s)
forget (v)	oublier
fresh	frais
Friday	vendredi
fridge	réfrigérateur
friend	ami
full	plein
furniture	meubles

G

game	jeu
gate	barrière
generous	généreux
get (v)	1. avoir, obtenir 2. devenir
get dressed (v)	s'habiller
get up (v)	se lever
give (v)	donner
glasses	des lunettes
glove	gant
go (v)	aller
grandfather	grand-père
grandmother	grand-mère
grandparents	grands-parents
great	super
ground floor	rez-de-chaussée
guess (v)	deviner
guy	type, homme

H

handsome	beau
happy	heureux
hat	chapeau
have fun (v)	s'amuser

hear (v)	entendre
heavy	lourd
high	haut
holiday(s)	vacances
homework	devoirs
horrible	horrible
horse	cheval
horse-ride (v)	faire du cheval
horse riding	équitation
hot	très chaud
hour	heure
hungry (be)	avoir faim
hurt (v)	1. faire mal, 2. avoir mal
husband	mari

I

ice cream	glace
ice-skate (v)	faire du patin à glace
improve (v)	améliorer
interesting	intéressant
in love	amoureux
iron (v)	repasser

J

January	janvier
July	juillet
jump over (v)	sauter par-dessus
jumper	pull-over
June	juin

K

key	clé
kick (v)	donner un coup de pied
kind	gentil
kitchen	cuisine
knife (knives)	couteau(x)
know (v)	savoir, connaître

L

lamb	agneau
land (v)	atterrir
laugh (v)	rire
laser printer	imprimante laser
last	dernier(ère)
last month	*le mois dernier*
last night	*la nuit dernière*
last week	*la semaine dernière*
last year	*l'année dernière*
late	tard
lawyer	avocat (métier)
lazy	fainéant
leaf (leaves)	feuille(s)
learn (v)	apprendre
leather	cuir
leave (v)	partir, laisser, quitter
left	gauche
library	bibliothèque
like (v)	aimer
light	1. lumière 2. léger, clair *(adjectif)*
light-haired	châtain clair (cheveux)
listen to music (v)	écouter de la musique
living room	salon
look + *adj.* (v)	avoir l'air
look after (v)	s'occuper de (un malade, un enfant)
look for (v)	chercher
loud	fort, à haute voix
lose (v)	perdre
love (v)	aimer, adorer
low	bas

M

make (a bed) (v)	faire (un lit)
man (men)	homme(s)
map	carte, plan (géographique)
March	mars
mark	note
May	mai
medicine(s)	médicament(s)
meat	viande
meet (v)	rencontrer
milk	lait
mirror	miroir
mistake	erreur, faute
mobile phone	téléphone portable
Monday	lundi
money	argent
moon	lune
mother	mère
motorway	autoroute
mouse (mice)	souris
move (v)	bouger, déménager
movie	film

N

nap	sieste
near	près
need (v)	avoir besoin de
neighbour	voisin
nephew	neveu
nervous	anxieux, nerveux
never	jamais
nice	gentil, agréable
niece	nièce
noise	bruit
novel	roman
November	novembre

O

October	octobre
often	souvent

old	vieux
once	une fois
onion	oignon
open (v)	ouvrir

P

paint (v)	peindre
pair of scissors	paire de ciseaux
paper clip	trombone
parcel	colis
parrot	perroquet
party	soirée
patient	patient
PC / computer	ordinateur
pea	petit pois
pedestrian crossing	passage pour piétons
pen	stylo
pencil	crayon
phone (v)	téléphoner
phone	téléphone
picture	photo, image
pity	dommage
plane	avion
play (v)	jouer
play cards (v)	*jouer aux cartes*
play football, tennis (v)	*jouer au football, au tennis*
playroom	salle de jeux
playwright	dramaturge
plumber	plombier
pork	porc
postcard	carte postale
potato(es)	pomme(s) de terre
pretty	jolie
pupil	élève
put on (v)	mettre (un vêtement, des chaussures)

Q

queue (v)	faire la queue

R

rabbit	lapin
racket	raquette
rain	pluie
raincoat	imperméable
rarely	rarement
read (v)	lire
rent (v)	louer
reply	réponse
reply (v)	répondre
rest (v)	se reposer
ride a horse (v)	monter à cheval
right (be) (v)	avoir raison
right	droite
ring (v)	sonner
road	route
roof	toit
rude	grossier
ruler	règle (pour mesurer)

S

sad	triste
same	identique
Saturday	samedi
scared	effrayé
to be scared (v)	*avoir très peur*
scarf	écharpe, foulard
school bag	cartable
scissors	ciseaux
seat	siège, place (de théâtre, cinéma)
see (v)	voir
sell (v)	vendre
September	septembre
shave (v)	raser
shelf (shelves)	étagère(s)
shirt	chemise
shoe	chaussure
shop	magasin
short	court, petit
shout (v)	crier
shower	douche
sick	malade
silly	idiot, bête
sing (v)	chanter
single	célibataire
sister	sœur
ski (v)	skier
skirt	jupe
sky	ciel
sleep (v)	dormir
slipper	chausson
slim	mince
slow	lent
small	petit
smart	élégant (GB) / intelligent (US)
smoke (v)	fumer
snow	neige
sock	chaussette
sometimes	parfois
son	fils
soon	bientôt
sorry	désolé
spend (v)	1. dépenser de l'argent 2. passer du temps
stairs	escalier(s)
stamp	timbre
star	étoile
start (v)	commencer
stay (v)	rester

stop (v)	arrêter, s'arrêter
storm	tempête
story	histoire
straight	directement
street	rue
strong	fort
stupid	stupide
suit	costume
suitcase	valise
sun	soleil
Sunday	dimanche
surname	nom de famille
surprised	surpris
sweep (v)	balayer
swim (v)	nager

T

tail	queue
take (v)	prendre
take away (v)	emporter
take back (v)	reprendre (un objet)
take off (v)	1. décoller (pour un avion) 2. enlever (un vêtement, des chaussures)
talk (v)	parler
tall	grand
taxi, cab	taxi
tea	thé
tell (v)	dire, raconter
tell the truth (v)	*dire la vérité*
term	trimestre
thirsty (be)	avoir soif
Thursday	jeudi
tidy (v)	ranger
tie	cravate
today	aujourd'hui
together	ensemble
tomato	tomate
tomorrow	demain
tonight	ce soir, cette nuit
tooth (teeth)	dent(s)
towel	serviette de toilette
traffic	circulation
traffic jam	embouteillage
traffic light	feu de signalisation
travel (v)	voyager
trip	voyage
trousers	pantalon
tube, underground	métro
Tuesday	mardi
turn off (v)	éteindre (le chauffage, le gaz, la lumière)
turn on (v)	allumer (le chauffage, le gaz, la lumière)
twice	deux fois

U

ugly	laid
umbrella	chapeau
uncle	oncle
under	sous, en-dessous
understand (v)	comprendre
usually	d'habitude

V

vacuum (v)	passer l'aspirateur
veal	veau
vegetable	légume
visit (v)	visiter, rendre visite

W

wake up (v)	se réveiller
wall	mur
walk (v)	marcher
want (v)	vouloir
wash (v)	laver
wash the dishes / do the washing-up (v)	*faire la vaisselle*
watch (v)	regarder
watch TV	*regarder la télévision*
watch	montre
weak	faible
wear (clothes) (v)	porter (des vêtements)
weather	le temps (qu'il fait)
Wednesday	mercredi
wife	épouse
wild	sauvage
window	fenêtre
woman (women)	femme(s)
work (v)	1. travailler 2. marcher/ fonctionner (radio)
write (v)	écrire

Y

yesterday	hier
young	jeune

Z

zoo-keeper	gardien de zoo

INDEX

INDEX

Maquette couverture : Cécile Gallou. Maquette intérieure et mise en page : Al'Solo. Photogravure : laser graphie
L'impression de ce livre a été effectuée dans les ateliers de STIGE - Turin pour Albin Michel Éducation.
Achevé d'imprimer en JANVIER 2000. N° d'édition : 16791. Dépôt légal : JANVIER 2000.